Mimi said, "One of the city reporters has a piece in tomorrow's paper about a group of punks uptown terrorizing an old Jewish lady who's a concentration camp survivor. Tyler thinks this group is tied to a bigger group out West somewhere, Idaho or Washington State, and he thought it'd be just nifty if I went out and poked around. It took me a week to convince him that those creeps kill FBI and IRS agents just for sport. Imagine sending a cute little Colored girl to ask them why they act so ugly?"

Mimi was still pissed at the memory of Tyler's insistence that she'd probably be perfectly safe. "Then, a couple of our Ladies of the Evening who'd been stringing me along for months with the promise of a blockbuster of a story disappeared on me. Just vanished into their nighttime." Mimi shrugged and poured herself another glass of sangria.

Gianna heard the shattering sound of her world colliding with Mimi's. If she'd been alone she'd have asked, yelled, *"Why? Why must Mimi be looking for missing prostitutes and evil-doing skinheads?"*

This novel is a work of fiction. All locales are used fictitiously. Names, characters, and incidents are a product of the author's imagination, and any resemblance to actual events or persons, living or dead, is coincidental.

NIGHT SONGS

A GIANNA MAGLIONE MYSTERY

BY PENNY MICKELBURY

The Naiad Press, Inc.
1995

Copyright © 1995 by Penny Mickelbury

All rights reserved. No part of this book may be reproduced or transmitted in any form or by any means, electronic or mechanical, including photocopying, without permission in writing from the publisher.

Printed in the United States of America on acid-free paper
First Edition

Edited by Katherine V. Forrest
Cover design by Bonnie Liss (Phoenix Graphics)
Typeset by Sandi Stancil

Library of Congress Cataloging-in-Publication Data

Mickelbury, Penny, 1948–
    Night songs : a Gianna Maglione mystery / by Penny Mickelbury.
        p.   cm.
    ISBN 1-56280-097-3
    I. Title.
PS3563.I3517N54   1995
813'.54—dc20   94-41091
                                                          CIP

This and all work is dedicated with love and gratitude to my family, whose love and support is the wind beneath my wings:
Louise, AJ and Cynthia, Helen and Bill, Dianne, Niki, Genie; and to the Gentlewomen in Virginia
who gave me a room of my own in which to write.

About the Author

Penny Mickelbury is a former Washington, DC newspaper, radio and television reporter. A committed free spirit, she has lived in New York, Chicago, California, and is back in Washington, teaching and writing. She is the author of *Keeping Secrets*. *Night Songs* is the second in the Gianna Maglione/Mimi Patterson mystery series. She is currently at work on a novel of historical fiction and a collection of short stories.

I

High heels click-clacked on the cracked pavement — stiletto, spike, the highest-of-the-high heels —
extensions of long shapely legs made longer by the
abbreviated and skin-tight black spandex dress. The
woman was what she appeared to be: hooker, whore,
prostitute, trick baby, shady lady, bitch. She'd been
called all of those names applied to women who
exchanged sex for money. She'd been called most of
them within the last hour by a pitiful excuse for a
man who blamed her because no matter how hard
they both tried, he remained limp. And then he'd

called her the names, loudly and violently and with a deep hatred, as if people like her didn't have feelings that could be hurt. Then, finally, expectedly, he'd called her "stupid nigger cunt."

"If I'm such a piece of shit, and you're here with me, what does that make you?" she'd finally snarled. And he'd hauled off and hit her, punched her right in the stomach. And she'd kicked him in his flaccid balls, then delivered a perfectly placed right hook to his weak chin, laying him out on the dusty floor. "You got a lot of nerve calling me names, you pitiful piece of poor white trash!" And with that she'd grabbed his pants, her shoes, jacket and purse, and run like hell, out of the seedy New York Avenue motel and into the chilly, early spring night, wishing as she always did that if white men couldn't stay at home, they could at least leave their venom there. She was so weary of the self-hatred they inevitably visited upon her, and women like her, as if punishing them would somehow absolve the men of the misery that was their lives. And at these times she was always ambivalent in her feelings about their wives, vacillating between pity that they must put up with such jerks, and believing that anybody stupid enough to marry one of these fools deserved whatever she got.

In an alley two and a half blocks and a world away from the motel, between a twenty-four-hour gas station and a twenty-four-hour carry-out, she quickly put on her fuzzy mohair jacket, shoes and stockings, re-arranged the cinnamon-brown real-hair wig, and counted the money in the creep's wallet. She whispered a silent prayer of thanks for the three hundred dollars that would allow her to go home and

2

get a decent night's sleep for a change. She'd even be able to wake up early enough to feed and dress her daughter and send her off to second grade with a hug and a kiss, like all good mothers do. As a gesture of the gratitude she felt, which was part of her emerging new spiritual awareness, after she'd wiped the creep's wallet and its contents clean of her fingerprints (for like many in her profession she was not unknown to the police department) she tossed it — credit cards and all — into the garbage dumpster, instead of selling the cards to her pal, Bo, as she'd once have done. American Express and Visa Gold — those cards were worth extra. But what the hell . . .

Now, here she was, safe and free and walking aimlessly on a tree-lined residential street, comforted by the silent, dark houses in which normal people were doing normal things, like drinking beer and eating chips and watching television and falling asleep. This was not a neighborhood of the wealthy: the houses were small and the vehicles in the driveways utilitarian. But all was neat and clean and so very well-cared for: perfectly clipped grass and hedges; doors and windows symmetrically aligned and adorned; the presence of children's games and toys at virtually every house indicative of proper nurturing; several of the yards bearing evidence of early spring fertilizing and planting. Her own mother had just the previous weekend deemed the soil soft enough for tilling and liming. She felt almost like she could be one of them in that moment, unfettered by the need to attract paying customers, overcome by the normality of it all.

Enveloped by the night, the clickety-clack of the

stiletto heels was the only real proof that she strolled there, inside the shadows. Since she wore all black, including her skin, the deep darkness of the still night became part of her wardrobe. Somewhere in her consciousness was the understanding that she'd have to return to the bright lights and action of New York Avenue to find a taxi. But most of her mind, when she let go of the anger and pain of the creep's words, was on the decision taking shape and form there. Actually, she'd made the decision earlier in the day; but since night was her strong time, the time when she thought most clearly, when she could take action, she strolled, releasing the tension and finding comfort in the increasing chill of the night. She walked herself through the mental exercises and reaffirmed her decision. She checked her watch: just past midnight by the luminous digital read-out. Not too late to call, she decided.

She turned a corner, angling toward the main drag and a taxi, and spied a lighted phone booth. She crossed New York Avenue against the light and had to scamper the last few steps to avoid being nailed by a pizza delivery truck. She shot the driver a "fuck you" with one hand while the other burrowed deep inside the huge, black leather bag in search of a small notepad. She was rehearsing what she'd say, how she would tell part of the story but withhold some of the juicy details in hopes of making a few dollars, even though the woman already said flat out she didn't pay money for information.

How to make money without selling her body was the new thought that filled her mind so that she did not hear the car that drew up to her from behind — a shiny, new black Jeep Wrangler with the top off a full month too early; did not feel it ease past her and slow to a crawl; did not see the man in the passenger seat turn and nod to the one who sat behind him; did not see, until it was too late, the shiny object spinning end over end toward her. And in truth, had she seen it in time, she would not have recognized it nor could she have prevented it from finding its designated home. The expertly hurled hunting knife lodged in her chest, just below the clavicle, and penetrated her heart. The look of confused surprise that spread across her face died with her, but not before the sound that was in her throat struggled to live: "I know about you!" she cried out. But the men didn't hear. They turned up the music as the Jeep was shifted into high gear and disappeared into the night. The song was one of death.

Way down and all the way across town from the northeast end of New York Avenue, across the Anacostia River, deep within Southeast Washington, inside a tiny brick row house, a second-grader cried out in her sleep, flinging her arms wildly, waking her grandmother who grabbed the child to her bosom and uttered her own, quieter cry, one born of a fear not defined but all too well understood.

Closer to the stilled stilettoes, but yet far enough away to make a huge difference in rent, in another darkened bedroom, Gianna Maglione also cried out, but not from inside the distress of a bad dream. She was powerless to control her responses to the mouth and touch of her lover, Mimi Patterson, and Mimi's mouth was, at the moment, lodged hungrily between Gianna's legs and she could only cry out in the joy of release. She could hear her own heartbeat, feel it pushing and pounding within her chest even as her body relaxed, tension ebbing. She felt Mimi wipe her mouth on the sheet, then felt her crawl up the bed and lie close beside, her head on Gianna's breast listening to her heart. Gianna plunged her hands into the wild, curly mass of Mimi's hair and whispered in her ear. Mimi shivered and sighed. A gust of chilly night air rushed into the slightly opened window, rattling the tiny-slatted blinds, bringing with it snatches of Sarah Vaughan from the neighbors' stereo.

The moon hung high and luminous in the inky sky. Gunshots vibrated, dogs howled, sirens split the air. Life and death, love and hate, beauty and evil — all danced to the songs of the night as another April night in the Nation's capital ticked its way into memory.

Herman Bashinski was sweating bullets. It was not a phrase the computer salesman would have used to describe his current predicament; rather, it was how the homicide detective would have described the scene before him, had he been asked, as he watched Herman try, for the fourth time, to explain that no, he did not know a woman named Shelley Kelley, nor did he know a man named George Thomas, and he most certainly had been at home with his family on Friday night past. If the police didn't believe him they could ask his wife. And Herman, for the fifth time, wiped his high-domed, freckled forehead with his now-damp handkerchief and tried to act belligerent, the way upstanding citizens do when their most sacred, God-given rights are being trampled upon.

The door to the interview room opened and a uniformed officer ushered in a small, tidy, mocha-colored man who took several appropriately small and tidy steps into the room and stood before Herman. George Thomas looked from Herman to the detective and back to Herman.

"That's him, Detective. Elijah, the night porter, had to lend him a pair of pants, and then help him break into his car. Green 1992 Chrysler LeBaron, Maryland license 2009 ZQ. And of course, there was no tip for Elijah because the gentleman had no wallet."

And with those words, George Thomas stepped carefully and distastefully away from Herman and the detective, folded his arms across his chest, and waited, either to be allowed to leave, or for questions. He had no pity for Herman and no liking for the police. He knew they thought him little better than the hookers and pimps and johns that frequented his motel and paid for the barren, musty rooms by the hour. He knew that despite the elegant perfection of his hand-tailored silk and wool navy blue suit, cream-colored linen shirt, cordovan calf slip-ons, the police and the Hermans of the world saw only a

7

Black man who catered to low-lifes. But George Thomas had the memory of truth to fuel his existence.

He remembered the day forty-three years ago when he and his dearly departed Rachel bought the motel on New York Avenue, right on the major route from New York City to points South, to the original homes of most of the Blacks who now lived in the Northeast. It was a time when Black families en route to or from visiting kin in New York or in Georgia kept his rooms full year round because they could not, in those days, book rooms in Holiday Inns and Howard Johnsons. They kept the rooms full and the restaurant busy day and night, winter and summer, and made him a wealthy man. But times changed, and so did New York Avenue, and so did the people who needed his rooms. And his Rachel, God rest her, was gone. So he had drained the pool and closed the restaurant and removed the televisions and the oil paintings from the rooms and accommodated his paying customers: What they wanted was a bed and a toilet, not a home away from home. But George Thomas still ran a clean establishment, just like in the old days, and he paid close attention to who came and went and he had a nose for trouble. So when Shelley Kelley came barrelling down the hallway barefoot, orange wig sideways on her head, her shoes and some clothes in one hand, and dragging behind her the monstrous black purse that women of her profession seemed to prefer, George quickly grabbed the .357 Magnum — for which he had a license — from his desk drawer and waited. And finally, after almost half an hour, Herman Bashinski crept down the hall and around the corner and motioned to George.

"Psst. Hey, Buddy. C'mere a minute, would ya?"

"What do you want?" asked George coldly, not moving.

"I just need to talk to you for a minute, that's all."

"About what?" George fingered the trigger of the heavy gun.

"I need your help!" Herman whined piteously and stepped cautiously around the corner, pudgy pink legs tightly together, dingy yellow boxer shorts chafing. That's when George realized what Shelley Kelley had carried in her other hand along with her shoes. She'd been moving too fast for him to see clearly.

"What do you want?" asked George again.

"Some pants. And some help getting my car started. My keys are in my pants and my pants are . . ." Herman abandoned the explanation, sweat popping out on his head.

George Thomas was five feet four inches tall; but even if he shared Herman's lofty six feet he'd not have given him a pair of his pants. Showing no movement detectable by Herman, George used his foot to press a button under the counter and in less than half a minute, a tall, well-built, but elderly man appeared behind Herman and when he spoke, Herman jumped.

"Yessir, Mr. Thomas?" Elijah said softly.

"Help him if you can and if you wish." And George said no more; indeed, paid no more attention to Herman and his problems.

George Thomas did not like this man nor those

9

like him, suburban white people who came into D.C. specifically to break the law — to buy drugs or women or weapons — and then to return to their safe, clean communities and point accusingly at the Sodom that was the Nation's capital. George Thomas did, however, like Shelley Kelley. He was an observant man, and an excellent judge of character. He was always correct when he assessed a young woman as being "wrong" for the work of the prostitute. He had advised Shelley to make a better life for herself, and was as proud as any father when he learned that she'd attached herself to some group that taught her how to do yoga and meditation and be a vegetarian. George didn't understand exactly what it was all about and he didn't need to; what mattered was that this bright, vivacious young girl was getting out of the street life. So when he heard that Shelley Kelley's body had been found eight blocks away with a hunting knife in her chest, he called the police and gave them Herman Bashinski's description and the license number of his car.

"So Herman," drawled the detective. "You wanna tell us about this here Shelley Kelley?" He leaned back and balanced himself on the chair's two rear legs and watched Herman's face work.

"I . . . I already told you. I don't know anybody by that name."

Irritated, the detective let the chair fall on its front legs with a thud and in a single motion, reached to the folder on the table before him, snapped it open, and whipped out a glossy black and white photograph which he shoved toward Herman. "You tellin' me you don't know her, Herman?"

"No. I mean yes. I mean, I never knew her name.

Not really. You know, you don't exactly get acquainted . . ." Herman's voice trailed off and he wiped the sweat from his face again and told the detective the whole story, from the beginning, including how he was unable to have an erection and how he'd punched the whore and how she'd kicked him and then run off with his pants.

And because the police had already found Herman's pants and wallet in the dumpster, the detective believed his story, told him to keep his sorry, limp dick at home, told him and George to beat it. And that left the weary homicide detective without a single lead in his investigation of the murder of one Shelley Kelley because if Herman Bashinski didn't kill her the detective didn't know who did and he really didn't have the energy to care. This was his ninth murder this week, the thirteenth in his open and active case file. And she was just a hooker.

Carolyn King stood stonily dry-eyed watching the two policewomen search her daughter's bedroom. *They're just about Sandra's age,* she thought, as they calmly stripped away every vestige of her daughter's privacy. Carolyn had never interfered with or searched Sandra's things and it was uncomfortable for her to watch two total strangers do what she'd never done.

"Did your daughter have an address book or a diary, Mrs. King?" asked one of the officers as she emptied the contents of the desk drawers onto the desk top.

"That kind of thing she kept with her. In that big, black purse she carried with her everywhere," said Carolyn King dully, looking at the stacks of envelopes and piles of papers held by rubber bands and paper clips, and remembering how neat and orderly Sandra was, even as a girl.

"Who were Shelley's friends, Mrs. King?" The second officer piled a stack of clothes from the closet on the bed and began sifting through them, checking the pockets. These were the normal clothes, the jeans and slacks and shirts and dresses that Sandra wore around the house, to the store, and, on occasion, to church.

Carolyn looked blankly at the officer, her face saying what her mouth could not: *Why are you asking me about this Shelley?*

"Who did she hang out with, Mrs. King? Where? Did she hang with old high school friends? Who?" The officer struggled not to sound bored, not to show the irritation she was feeling with the woman whose blank, dry eyes stared at her.

"You mean Sandra?" asked her mother.

"She used the name Shelley Kelley on the street."

And that's when Carolyn King broke. "My daughter's name is Sandra Ann King! That's what I named her! That's what it says on her birth certificate! I don't know nothin' about no Shelley Kelley!" And Carolyn King rushed from her dead daughter's bedroom into the small, neat living room and sank into the new sofa that Sandra had recently bought for her and cried for every one of the twenty-two years her only daughter had wasted.

* * * * *

12

Lt. Giovanna Maglione stood up from her desk and stretched every inch of her lithe, five foot-eight-inch frame, arms high above her head, back arched almost in half. That she was in the tenth hour of what would likely be a fourteen-hour day had no negative effect on the starched crispness of her white shirt and the sharpness of the crease in her black slacks. Her tie was still perfectly in place, as was her wild mane of heavy, mahogany hair: twisted into thick ropes on either side of her head and held firmly in place with ivory barrettes that once belonged to her great-grandmother. She rubbed her clear, hazel eyes, tired from the hours of staring at the computer screen; rotated her neck; did a set of deep knee bends; and breathed deeply in and out for sixty seconds. None of it could remove all of the tension stored in her body, nor could it compensate for the lack of sleep; but she revived enough to continue work on the monthly crime report and analysis due on her boss's desk at 8:00 a.m. sharp — which was in about eleven hours. She knew with absolute certainty that Inspector Eddie Davis, head of the Intelligence Division of the Washington, D.C. Police Department and her immediate boss, would not tolerate her being even one minute late. Not because he was an unreasonable or unkind man, but because he had warned her time and again about participating in her investigations instead of directing them, and when she'd persisted he'd issued a direct order: behave in a manner befitting a lieutenant or else. The "or else" was looking better and better. The only benefit to being a lieutenant as far as she was concerned was being the boss: She was head of the three year-old Hate Crimes Unit.

Seven of Washington's finest — including herself — bore the responsibility of bringing to justice those who would violate the legal and civil rights of persons based on race, religion or sexual orientation. But hate was big business in D.C., as well as in most of America, much too big for six dedicated but grossly overworked cops to contain. So, bucking the established order and incurring its wrath, she frequently joined her team in the street investigating crimes of hatred. And because she did, she usually was late submitting the paperwork required of those who held the rank of lieutenant and above, of those elevated to the level of "white shirt," which separated the high-ranking cops from the rank and file who wore blue shirts. Not that she often wore the shirt or the uniform. She had it on today because she'd been summoned to testify before a committee of the City Council. She put a stopper in the feeling of anger and frustration that such appearances always generated and returned to her seat behind the desk and the crime report on the computer screen.

She looked up at the sound of a knock at her door. Familiar with the modus operandi of the Chief and of her boss, she waited for the door to open and for one of them to stick his head in. When instead there came a second knock, she frowned and called out, "Come on in." The door opened to admit an attractive woman of about thirty-five wearing a well-cut, form-fitting cranberry knit dress, and, pinned to the collar, the ID badge of the civilian employee of the Police Department.

"Sorry to disturb you, Lieutenant, but I knew you were still here and I need to talk to you."

"Have a seat." Gianna gestured to the leather

armchair at the corner of her desk and watched the woman approach, watched her make up her mind even as she sat down that she would, in fact, say what she'd come to say.

"I'm sorry I don't know how to pronounce your name. I've heard it said but I just don't remember."

Gianna laughed easily, putting the woman immediately at ease.

"Don't worry. The chief can't pronounce it either and I've known him for twenty years. What can I do for you?"

"My name is Gwen Thomas and I work in records, which doesn't have anything to do with why I'm here ..." She stopped, stared down at her perfectly manicured nails which were the same color as her dress, took a deep breath, and continued. "I've read about you, about your cases, and I hear people in the building talk about you. They say you're one of the real people."

Gianna didn't speak but held the woman's dark, sad eyes with her own calm, clear, hazel ones and waited.

"My sister got killed two months ago. She was a hooker and a drug addict. Not one of your upstanding citizens, I know, but she was my sister and she was murdered and she didn't deserve to die. Not like she did." Overcome now by emotion and struggling to control the tears that formed and dripped, she stopped again, staring again at the hands folded tightly in her lap.

"Did you come to me because you don't think the police are handling the investigation properly?" In D.C., as in other big cities, poor people, and especially poor people of color, believed they got short

15

shrift from an over-burdened justice system, and they quite often were correct. Perhaps Gwen Thomas thought that her proximity to the department might get better results.

"Didn't you say once that crimes against women were hate crimes, too, just like crimes against Jews or Black people or gay people?" She was in control now, pain replaced by anger, and Gianna knew this was no bullshit visit by a disgruntled citizen.

"Yes, I said that." She leaned across the desk, closing the distance to Gwen Thomas.

"My sister was killed because she was a woman. Because she was a hooker. Three more were killed, just like she was —"

"What do you mean, just like she was?" Gianna asked, and she knew deep within herself that the answer would spell trouble.

"Somebody threw a knife at her. A big hunting knife, not a kitchen knife. Threw it in her chest."

Gianna's heart raced, her stomach dropped and her brain buzzed as she visualized the scene.

"You're telling me that four women — all prostitutes — have been killed by hunting knives thrown into them?" Gianna wasn't easily or often surprised so she didn't cover it well, or recover from it quickly, and Gwen Thomas misunderstood.

"That's exactly what I'm telling you and if you don't believe me you can ask those stupid motherfuckers in Homicide!"

"I believe you, Miss Thomas." And, Gianna thought, I also know which stupid motherfuckers in Homicide you mean. "And I fully understand your anger. But I need for you to very calmly tell me everything you know, beginning with your sister's murder."

The murdered Andrea Thomas had begun life as a good girl, graduated from high school and secretarial school, got married, got a job, had a baby. Smoked crack. Once. To experiment. A year later, at the age of twenty-five, she was out on the street selling her body to support her habit. In rare moments of lucidity she professed her love for her husband and child and family and pledged to restore her life. But Gwen Thomas didn't know of anyone who had successfully kicked crack and she didn't expect her baby sister to be the exception to the rule.

"I wasn't holding my breath waiting for her to change. I used to drive by places where I knew she hung out, just to make sure she had clothes and food. I didn't like her life but it wasn't my place to judge her. She was my baby sister and I loved her."

About a month ago, Gwen Thomas said, she began searching for her sister in all her known haunts. Nobody had seen Andrea. Nobody knew anything. Three or four nights a week she searched, becoming more and more worried and frightened. Finally, standing at the mouth of an alley under a high intensity street light designed to deter crime, she held up a twenty dollar bill and promised it to the first person who told her where to find Andrea. An hour later she was on the grounds of D.C. General Hospital, in the shadow of the city jail, at the morgue, identifying Jane Doe 23-1993 as Andrea Thomas Willoughby, who'd been there for three weeks, waiting to be identified and claimed.

"I thought she ODed, but when this morgue

person told me, almost by accident, that she was found with this big knife sticking out of her chest, I damn near peed on myself. Last time Andrea was rational enough to have a normal conversation, which was back in April, she told me that her good friend Sandra King had just gotten killed that same way. And then at the funeral last week — at Andrea's funeral — another girl told me the same thing happened to two other girls." Gwen Thomas seemed to be reliving the moment that she realized her sister's death was but one thread in a larger fabric.

"My sister did some wrong things in her life, Lieutenant, but if the people she hurt the most still loved her, no damn body had the right to kill her."

And with that, Gwen Thomas shook hands with the woman she believed would avenge her sister's murder, and returned to the computer terminal where she searched out citizens with overdue parking tickets and sent them notices explaining that the original fine had now doubled or tripled, leaving Lt. Maglione staring at her own computer terminal but seeing large knives protruding from the bodies of women hated because they used their bodies to bring pleasure to those who hated them.

II

Mimi Patterson stepped off the wonderfully air-conditioned MetroBus and into the miserable, muggy, mid-day heat at Thomas Circle and walked north up 13th Street to P Street, then east toward 9th Street. In less than a block she was the only woman walking the street whose profession that activity was not. Not that there was any danger of confusion: even in her midriff-baring T-shirt, tight Levis, and leather sandals, she wore too many clothes to be mistaken for a professional. She strolled casually, noticing how dramatically — and how quickly — the block changed from the beautifully landscaped circle with General Thomas (she didn't remember who he was or why he had his own monument) astride his bronze mare at 13th Street, to the grungy, scraggly section four blocks away at 9th Street.

Mimi hoped that her attire and her demeanor would mark her as a neighborhood resident — trendy, upwardly mobile — and not as the newspaper reporter that she was, in search of what she felt was a potentially big story involving prostitutes. She refused to remind herself that she really didn't know what kind of story she was chasing, because the two women who'd been stringing her along for months with the promise of something big had disappeared from their regular beats. She knew that prostitutes worked specific areas, like drug dealers, and she knew she was in the wrong neighborhood. What she didn't know was how to find somebody who apparently didn't want to be found since hookers didn't leave forwarding addresses. And she almost succeeded in convincing herself that it wasn't really so wild a shot to think that women who worked one side of town might be acquainted with women from another side . . .

As she strolled, she became aware of a car inching along beside her. She stopped and turned to face the vehicle, and the automatic window on the passenger side slid down to give her a good look at the overweight, middle-aged man in dark glasses who leaned over and spoke casually, almost too casually.

"Wanna party?"

"What?" she said, so genuinely confused that the full implication of his meaning — and the anger it roused in her — didn't kick in immediately. And when it did, she was too astounded to reply, so she reached into her back pocket and extracted a small pen and notepad and walked to the rear of the car and wrote down the number of the Virginia license plate. Must have been the day for slow responses because she'd written the entire number before he slammed his foot on the accelerator and screeched off down the block, leaving an impressive amount of rubber on the hot pavement.

"You slimy son of a bitch!" she yelled at the disappearing car. "You piece of shit bastard!" But her anger disappeared as fast the object of it, and Mimi was left holding something that resembled hatred. She knew there was no logical reason or way to mistake her for a prostitute; but there was also no mistaking her Blackness. And the white man saw a Black woman and reached what for him was a logical conclusion. She hated him and people like him and all the forces of evil and ugly that had conspired over time to allow him to think he had the right to make such an assumption about her. And she hated the circumstances that had brought her to this location in search of women — most of whom would certainly be Black — about whom she would make a similar assumption. And for a moment all feeling drained from her and she took a few deep breaths to restore herself, leaving behind the bitter bile of hatred, reclaiming only what she needed to get her job done.

She scanned the block hoping, praying to recognize one of the women she knew from previous interviews; but when she recognized no one, she looked for a woman she thought it safe to approach. The combination of crack, AIDS, and a harsh economy, made prostitutes a generally unfriendly and unapproachable group, unless of course money was involved. Her newspaper's policy absolutely forbade paying for information, but many investigative reporters weren't beyond passing a buck or two to a good source. Just a way of saying thanks. So Mimi dug in her pocket and extracted several bills. She had, she knew, the covert attention of at least three women. Making a quick but informed judgment, she walked briskly up to a woman who stood slightly apart from two others and leaned against the bus stop.

"I'm not a cop, I'm a newspaper reporter," she said, the money clearly visible in her hand, speaking quietly so only the woman would hear, "and the only thing I want from you is help finding some friends. Okay?" Mimi waited. Only the woman's eyes moved, from Mimi's face to the money in her hand.

"Do you know Shelley Kelley or Starry Knight?" Mimi waited again, and again the woman remained motionless.

"I'm going to drop this money — it's about fifteen dollars — in the front yard of the last house on this block. You ask around and find Shelley and Starry for me and there's another twenty in it for you. I'll wait for you on the bench at the Thomas Circle bus stop this same time next week."

This time Mimi didn't wait for the woman's response. She turned and walked back the way she came, casually, calmly, until she reached the corner. Then she stumbled and reached out to grab a spike of the wrought iron fence that enclosed the front yard of the last house on the block to steady herself.

The two prostitutes who Mimi had passed up watched her turn south at 13th Street and disappear.

Fourteen-year-old Sweet Meat strolled over to her fifteen-year-old pal, Marilyn Monroe, and blew cigarette smoke into his face. He choked, slapped her lightly, and they both moved nearer to Baby Doll who was nineteen but looked at least twice that.

"What the hell did she want?" Sweet said sullenly.

"Who the hell is she?" demanded Marilyn. Baby didn't say anything for a long moment. Then she straightened her voluminous wig, smoothed her skirt, checked her seams, moistened her lips.

"They'll let anybody outta the Police Academy these days."

"That pitiful chile 'sposed to be a *cop*?" Marilyn was both incredulous and suspicious. "Didn't look like no cop to me. Clothes too clean for her to be undercover. And she don't walk like no cop."

"Maybe you didn't hear me the first time. I asked you what did she want." Sweet was now hostile as well as sullen, which had no effect at all on Baby who held advanced degrees in hostile and sullen from the Graduate School of Hard Knocks. She was busy formulating a plan in that part of her mind still left functioning by the heroin to which she'd been addicted since she was fourteen, a plan for retrieving the money lying in the front yard of the last house on the block without being noticed by Sweet and Marilyn.

"She asked me if I knew some people. Two girls work over on the Northeast side, she said. Said she couldn't find 'em over there and thought they might be over here. Show you how stupid she is. Over here on the Northwest side lookin' for somebody from 'cross town." And Baby flung her mass of Diana Ross-like hair at the thought of such ignorance.

"How come you didn't tell her something, anything," whined Sweet in an abrupt change of mood. "That way you coulda got the money."

"I stopped talkin' to the police when I was thirteen. Don't never say nothin' to 'em, don't care how much money they offer." Baby looked up into the cloudless sky. "Time for me to go home and get some rest. See y'all tonight." And she followed in Mimi's steps.

"She can be a real bitch sometimes," said Marilyn, and the two of them strolled east on P Street. Had they gone the opposite way, had they followed Baby, they would have seen her drop her purse just before reaching the corner, exactly at the place where Mimi had stumbled just moments before.

"What is wrong with you guys?" Lieutenant Maglione was comfortable voicing her frustration with her superior officers, though she wished it were unnecessary. She held the lowest rank of any police official in the room, was one of only three women, and was weary of having the same old discussions and arguments. The Captains, Inspectors, Deputy Chiefs, and Assistant Chiefs at the table kept their eyes respectfully on her though she detected some uneasy shifting.

"Why can't you accept crimes against women as hate crimes?" She pointed to the statistical crime report that lay before each of them, the innocuous-appearing quarterly document that rubbed their collective noses in the truth that the cops were losing the war against crime in D.C.

24

"Four women are dead. Prostitutes. A knife to the chest thrown — *thrown* mind you — from a passing car." She leaned back in her chair and pointed to Assistant Chief Ron Hampton. "If all the victims were Black and killed in the same way, you'd accept it as a hate crime." Then she turned to Inspector Mark Seltzer, head of Internal Affairs. "If they were all Jewish you'd accept it as a hate crime." She spread her hands flat out before her on the table and looked directly into the chief's eyes, intentionally avoiding eye contact with the one man present whom she knew to be homosexual. "If they were all homosexual, you'd all agree it was a hate crime. But they're all women. And not your version of nice women at that, and so you all just shrug your shoulders."

"That's not fair, Maglione, or correct."

She returned the steady, direct gaze of the Chief of Police, the man who'd been her mentor since her days at the training academy, and who still butchered her name with his hard, anglicized pronunciation of the soft Italian sounds. Half a dozen years as chief had done nothing to curb his overdrive energy, to lessen his intensity. He always complained that now he spent his time going to lunches and dinners and giving speeches instead of catching criminals, but he was every bit as tough now as when he was head of Homicide and later head of the Criminal Investigations Division. He was, and would always be, a street cop.

The Chief continued, "You're here at this meeting because some of us have questions about how to handle this case and we wanted you ..."

She grinned at him, shaking her head. "I'm here

at this meeting because I heard rumblings about some knife-throwing Daniel Boone killer of women and I badgered the hell out of Vincenzo until he gave me the deep and skinny and then I bullied my way in here."

Homicide chief Vince Pelligrino winced, eyes tightly shut, hands over his ears, vainly attempting to obliterate what he knew was coming.

"Tell 'em what you told me when I asked you about the Daniel Boone killings, Vincenzo," she said, her tone only half teasing. "Tell 'em how you said it was no big deal since it was only a couple of nobody hooker junkies."

"Lighten up, Maglione! *Che cosa fa!*" His use of Italian signaled to Gianna that she'd gone too far, that she'd offended him, and she apologized — *"Me scuse, Vincenzo"* — but didn't give up her quest to have the prostitute murders assigned to her Hate Crimes Unit.

"These are not ordinary homicides. These are crimes of hate. You know that's true." She looked around the table, watching her superiors watch her. None of them numbered among her close personal friends — except the chief — but she'd known them all for years, and she respected most of them. Still, sometimes she wondered what made them tick, how it was possible for them to be on the same side, have the same objectives, and yet differ so completely on such a fundamental issue: violence against women. "Four women are dead because some man — or some men — wanted power and control, not sex."

Vince Pelligrino sighed wearily. "Maglione, I got two hundred homicides already in this city and June ain't over yet. I could be looking at close to five hundred for the year. You wanna take the weight of some dead hookers, be my guest," he said, wiping his hands in an up and down movement that, in unspoken Italian, meant he washed his hands of the whole business. Then he looked quickly at the Chief. "That is if you don't see a problem with it."

The Chief shook his head and looked down the table at Inspector Eddie Davis, head of Intelligence under which the Hate Crimes Unit existed, who nodded his acquiescence, and finally toward the Vice guys, one of whom blew Gianna a kiss; the other shrugged that he didn't care one way or the other and shoved a box of files down the table toward her. She peered inside. The files looked raggedy and unkempt, like the Vice guys who worked the street, and she groaned inwardly. Yet another opportunity to play catch-up, to try and build a bias case from the mess that had been passed between Vice and Homicide for at least a year.

Washington, D.C. The head of the Hate Crimes Unit sat at her desk facing the window, looking out over her unique city, unlike any of its East Coast sister cities: smaller in land and population than Boston, New York, Newark, Philadelphia, Baltimore, Atlanta or Miami; smaller most certainly than the mid-Western and West Coast behemoths of Chicago or Detroit or Los Angeles or Houston. Unlike any American city — large or small — because, in reality, Washington was no city at all. It was the District of Columbia, the Nation's capital. The five hundred thousand or so citizens of the District of Columbia were disenfranchised in a way different from any other American citizens, and Gianna sometimes thought that was why policing the city was so difficult.

Until the early 1970s, the President of the United States appointed the mayor and the police chief and the other decision makers, and the Congress of the United States controlled the budget. These days, D.C. residents did elect their own mayor, and that mayor appointed the police chief, but the Congress still controlled the budget and most of the land within Washington — land that was home to the White House and the Capitol buildings and the dozens of monuments and museums and the hundreds of federal office buildings (IRS, FBI, HUD, HHS, etc) — none of which was taxable. Gianna could never consider this truth without wondering, seriously, whether the people in Congress truly understood the reason and intent of the Boston Tea Party. As much as Gianna disliked politics, she empathized with the mayor who was expected to find the resources to manage the crime while denied the right to tax most of the city's land. And Gianna felt just a little guilty because she had a lot more bad news for the mayor: Gianna believed there was a serial killer who preyed on prostitutes and she suspected that there were more than the four victims known by name to the police department.

Not only did the mayor not need to hear such daunting news, but the Chief did not want to be the bearer of such news; and that was why the Chief, who was appointed by the mayor, told the head of the Hate Crimes Unit, who was appointed by him, that he wanted all files and reports on the ill-named

"Daniel Boone killings" kept strictly confidential. Nobody but the Chief himself was to see the Daniel Boone files. That unnerved the head of Hate Crimes, because it meant withholding information from her boss. The Chief fully understood and sympathized with her trepidation, since he was withholding information from his own boss. But sometimes, he sagely informed his protege, life threw you a curve ball, and you had to catch the fucker barehanded.

III

"I oughta arrest 'em just for being the ugly, ignorant, evil pieces of shit that they are." Officer Cassandra Ali tossed her pretty head of baby dreadlocks and managed a crooked grin despite her anger, as her colleagues on the Hate Crimes Unit laughed at her pronouncement; but her boss saw beyond the grin to the venom that powered the words and was worried.

"Cassie! Don't be so cold! Give the dudes a chance." Officer Kenny Chang, the resident peacemaker, stepped easily into the role he normally played opposite Cassie, the resident cynic.

"Yeah, Cass, lighten up. After all, they haven't broken the law. Yet." Officer Robert Gilliam groaned and buried his head in his hands as he immediately recognized the failure of his attempt at sarcastic humor.

"What would make you happy, Bobby, for them to drag the old woman off to the gas chamber? Would that be breaking the law?" Officer Lynda Lopez bubbled and simmered, her anger like a pot about to boil over.

"Jeez, men are such assholes!"

"Oh, Cassie, come on. Not true and not fair."

"Shove it, Kenny. I'm tired of you trying to put a happy face on everything. What's happening to Sophie Gwertzman is a crime. You hear me, Bobby Gilliam? A crime!" Cassie stood up abruptly, knocking over her chair.

"Not on the books, Cass. We can call these guys all the names we want, but until they break the law . . ." Bobby held up his hands and shrugged.

"Then the law sucks." Cassie righted her chair and slumped into it.

"That's enough, guys." Detective Eric Ashby easily and competently gained control of his subordinates, while casting an uneasy glance across the room at his boss.

Gianna relished the time alone with her Team, secreted away in the cramped, crowded work room they called the Think Tank. She listened to them talk as she always did: leaning back in her chair, feet on the desk, eyes closed. She loved listening to them, feeling their intelligence and their energy and their dedicated but no-bullshit approach to law enforcement. She was proud of them. She believed them to be the best young cops in the Washington, D.C. police department. They worked for her because they wanted to: she had chosen them from a group of volunteers, police officers who wanted specifically to work in the newly created Hate Crimes Unit; young officers who knew they'd be doing a different kind of police work, who knew that along with the normal ugly that accompanied every crime, they'd have the added evil of hatred: hatred of a person because of race or color or religion or sexual orientation. She had chosen them because they were straight, gay, Black, white, Hispanic, Asian, male, female. She had chosen them because each of them, in some way, reminded her of herself at that age: idealistic and defiant and innocent and dedicated and a true believer in law as the great equalizer. To feel Cassie Ali's anger, to hear her scorn for the laws that protected victim as equally as victimizer, deeply worried Gianna.

"Did I miss something? I haven't seen a new report on the Gwertzman case." Gianna spoke quietly, evenly, directly to Cassie.

"This happened last night —"

"You weren't on duty last night."

"I know. Mrs. Gwertzman called me at home —"

"Called you at home?" Gianna bit off the words before Cassie completed her sentence, and the energy of the room shifted.

Gianna went icy when angered and not even Eric, who'd known her for twenty years, could withstand the glare of her anger. Cassie shifted uneasily, wisely allowing her self-righteous indignation to take a backseat. She scrunched down into her chair, managing to seem even younger and smaller than she was.

"Yes, Ma'am. I gave her my number in case ..."

"That's a violation of procedure. You have a beeper number to be reached out of shift. "

"Yes, Ma'am, but the old lady doesn't understand what it is or how it works, so I thought ..."

"You thought you could violate procedure when it suits your purposes?"

Cassie straightened herself, sitting as if at attention. "Lieutenant ... Anna ... they were playing concentration camp music outside her window at two in the morning. I heard it over the phone, that's how loud it was. She was hysterical when she called. She thought she was back in ... in ... that place."

Gianna allowed the silence to hang for a moment while she sought the balance between compassion and authority. Just as no parent would publicly claim any child as the favorite, neither would Gianna proclaim a favorite; but deep within she harbored a special care for Cassie, the one who was most like herself. Her own early years as a cop were marked by numerous rules violations because she believed that laws should bend to fit people, not the other way around. And the superior officer who had pulled her buns out of the fire more than once back then was the current Chief of Police and she remained grateful for his care and understanding because he was still pulling her buns out of the fire.

"There's an after hours noise ordinance —" Kenny began.

Cassie cut him off razor sharp and quick. "What

the hell good is a noise ordinance when psychological terrorism is the problem!"

"Cassie. All of you. Listen to me. We cannot impose morality. It has taken us this long in the development of our culture to determine that certain behavior generated by hatred violates people's basic rights, and that such behavior is criminal. But nowhere in the law does it say that hatred itself is a crime. The skinheads or Nazis or whoever they are, have a right to play Wagner at two in the morning — as long as they don't violate the noise ordinance. They even have a right to play it outside the home of a Buchenwald survivor —"

"But that's so wrong," Cassie wailed. "The woman is eighty years old, for Christ's sake!"

"Yes, it's wrong and it's evil and you've every right to every feeling that you're having. Just don't ever forget that you're a police officer with a duty to serve the rights of *all* citizens. Am I clear?"

The chorus of "Yes Ma'ams" floated gently in the room and dissipated the accumulated tension.

"Let's move on to another brand of depravity, shall we? Any word on those hunting knives?" Gianna asked Eric.

"Every major sporting goods, camping, and outdoor store on the East coast sells that knife. So do most military surplus stores." Eric shook his head in dismay. "But that's not the worst of it. Oh no. Not by a long shot."

Gianna tasted the bitterness of his words and sat and waited.

"There are no words to describe the condition of the files on these cases that we got from Homicide and Vice. Anna, you really gotta complain to the Chief —"

She held up her hand to silence him because she certainly would not join him in criticism of another division in the presence of subordinates. "What's in the files, Eric?"

"Who the hell knows?" Eric snarled. "I'm telling you, Boss, I've never seen anything like it. As far as I can tell, there's been almost no follow-up to leads. There are no forensic reports attached. Two of 'em don't even have autopsy reports attached. Hell, it even looks like somebody merged two of them, as if the two dead women were the same person. I can't tell which witness list goes with which file." Eric threw his hands up and then began pacing.

Gianna got up and crossed to the box containing the files. Each file bore the name of a victim, but it seemed that any semblance of order ended there. One by one she removed them and gave the file of each of the four murdered prostitutes to each of the four young cops before her. Remembering Gwen Thomas's pain and anger, she gave Andrea Thomas's file to Cassie.

"Do I need to tell you all what to do?" she asked, and before they could answer, she suggested that they get started.

She watched them leave and when the door closed she allowed herself to share Eric's anger about the condition of the files. "Did you talk to Pelligrino and —"

"Hell yes! And I'm sure you don't need for me to tell you how busy they are solving *real* murders. Too busy to worry about some dead hookers." When Eric was thoroughly angry all the blood drained from his face, making it stark white, making his red hair flame and his blue eyes glaciers. She watched him struggle for control. "What really pisses me off is those files look like they didn't care. It's just some hookers, so who cares, you know what I mean? And if I believe that —"

"McCreedy's back from vacation this week, isn't he?"

Eric frowned and nodded. "Why?"

"Because I want him to be a presence at Homicide and Vice until we're convinced that the victims' files are correct and complete. Because I want him to push and pull and prod until it becomes gently clear to Homicide and Vice that a victim's file is a victim's file whether or not they like the victim. Because I want to irritate them as they've irritated me and McCreedy is the best way I can think of to do that."

Tim McCreedy was as close to a perfect specimen of male pulchritude as Gianna had ever seen. He was six feet four inches tall. He had coal black hair and sea blue eyes and snow white teeth. He held national and international body building titles. He was a Black Belt in karate and had recently discovered the joys of kick boxing. And he was one hell of a good cop: detailed, organized, resourceful, and persistent to the point of being a pain in the ass when that was necessary. Tim McCreedy was also happily, openly, and joyously gay. Tim McCreedy was a flaming queen and proud of it. Tim McCreedy was despised by the macho cops of Homicide and Vice not only because he was a "fuckin' faggot," but because he had, on more than one occasion, beat the ever-lovin' shit out of every one of those macho cops stupid enough to call him a "fuckin' faggot" loud enough for him to hear. Now the macho boys would have to explain to Tim McCreedy how and why it was that the files on Andrea Thomas and Sandra King and Patricia MacIntyre and Rhonda Green were such a mess; would have to explain to the fuckin' faggot how they were just fuckin' whores . . .

"They're really gonna have it in for you for that," Eric said, his anger ebbing in the appreciation of the moment.

"I sincerely hope so," she said, still seething.

"Well, if anybody can find the missing pieces of those files, McCreedy's the man," Eric said.

"I just hope it's only four of them." She envisioned some dread-filled cop in Washington State and in California and in New York saying the same thing before each found more than a dozen prostitutes in each state, victims of a single serial killer. She couldn't bring herself to say out loud what she believed deep inside — that such a thing really was possible in D.C. — so she changed the subject.

"Nice job of diffusing the skinhead debate," she said.

Eric grinned his thanks and shook his head in amused wonderment. "That Cassie is a fierce little one. Those Nazi punks better watch their asses."

"It's our asses we'll need to worry about if she lets loose on one of them. I've never seen her so thrown out of balance."

"Do you want me to pull her from Gwertzman?"

"No, Eric, I don't think so. There may be another way to handle this."

Eric's antennae perked up at the tone in her voice and at the half-grin that raised her mouth at the corners. She picked up the phone, punched some numbers, and waited.

"Tyler Carson please."

Eric's eyes widened in disbelief. His boss calling the newspaper? She hated the media, despite the fact that her lover of a year was one of the best investigative reporters in town.

Those standing closest to Tyler's desk in the newsroom did a double take as he hung up one of the phones that he held, as he put down his copy editing pen, as he turned away from the computer monitor on which he was editing another story. Not one of them ever remembered seeing Tyler do only one thing at a time. He turned his back to the habitual crowd around an editor's desk and frowned his full attention into the phone.

"You will forgive the understatement if I acknowledge being totally surprised by this call."

Tyler Carson knew that Lt. Gianna Maglione was Mimi Patterson's lover. She knew he was gay and dating a married FBI agent. They both knew that Mimi would have a fit if she found out about this telephone call.

"This call is strictly off the record, Mr. Carson. Yes?"

"Of course." Tyler listened intently while Gianna related the terrorism inflicted upon eighty-year-old Sophie Gwertzman and why the police were powerless to make any arrests. He wrote down the names and addresses of those identified by Officer Cassandra Ali as being responsible and he wrote down Sophie

Gwertzman's address. Everything else he committed to memory, just as he had in his ace reporter days before he was city editor; and, like the best of journalists, he promptly erased from his mind the source of his information. When she was finished, Tyler asked, "Do you have a preference for which reporter is assigned this story?"

"I have a preference for which reporter is *not* assigned this story," Gianna answered as carefully as he'd asked, and hung up.

Baby Doll's feet hurt. She'd walked ten blocks out of her way in the ninety degree heat in her brand new purple spike heels so that she could meet the newspaper lady without being seen by any of her associates, and damned if that Marilyn Monroe wasn't standing right at the bus stop! Standing there in hot pink hotpants, holding up the pole like he didn't have a thing else in the world to do! Baby wondered if the newspaper lady had psyched her out and made an arrangement to meet Marilyn, too; but that question was answered when the bus arrived and the door opened and the fifth passenger off was the newspaper lady and she walked right past Marilyn without a hint of recognition to the bench where she was supposed to meet Baby. But Baby had no plans to move from the shadow of the apartment building that hid her from view unless and until Marilyn boarded that bus and evaporated, which he did; and when the bus was a full block away, Baby slowly — because her feet hurt — and cautiously — because she trusted not a living soul — approached the reporter from the rear, noticing for the first time how pretty she was.

"What's your name, Newspaper Lady?" Baby was impressed when the woman did not seem startled at being approached from behind. She didn't jump or make a noise but rather turned slowly to face Baby and smiled at her.

"My name is Montgomery Patterson."

"You got any ID?" Baby liked the woman's name, and she liked her voice and she liked that she wasn't skittish or nervous. Baby liked strong, tough women — especially ones like this one, a strong, tough Black woman who was also smart and educated and doing something for a living other than selling her body. She watched Mimi unzip and reach into a well-worn, black leather waist pouch and extract a handful of laminated identification cards that dangled from a chain, each of them bearing her photograph. Baby took her sweet time and scrutinized them one by one. She wished the numbers on the cards had some significance, because she could read numbers. She could not read words, so the markings on the cards conveyed no meaning. Certain, finally, that she'd masked her inability to read, she demanded, "Where's my twenty dollars?"

"Where's my information?" Mimi casually leaned back into the hard wooden bench and crossed her legs, her right knee poking through the hole in her jeans.

"What you wanna know?" Baby sat down next to Mimi and crossed her legs, too, black fishnet as far as you could see and then some.

"I wanna know where to find Shelley Kelley and Starry Knight."

"What you want with 'em?"

"That's not your concern."

"It is if you wanna do somethin' to hurt 'em. Just 'cause you work for the newspaper and not for the police don't make you Jesus Christ or a saint."

Mimi conceded the point. "They have some information for me, for a story, and I haven't been able to find them. They're not at any of their regular hangouts and nobody's seen them. I'm worried about them."

"You worried 'bout them or 'bout your story?"

"You're a tough Sister," Mimi said admiringly. "What's your name?"

"Damn right I'm tough. Got to be tough to work these streets. They call me Baby Doll out here but my name is Marlene. What kinda information was they gonna tell you?"

"I'm not sure," Mimi said slowly and honestly, remembering her conversations with the women she knew only as Shelley and Starry, for they'd refused to tell her their real names as Baby had just done so matter-of-factly. "I know it had something to do with big shot guys and hook . . . ah, prostitutes, but that's all I know."

Baby Doll snorted in disgust. "That ain't news. Big shot guys 'round here come a dime a dozen. Must be more'n that," Baby pried.

Mimi was growing annoyed and showed it. "Look, Baby, do you know where I can find Shelley and Starry or not?"

"Naw," Baby said offhandedly. "Never even heard of 'em."

"Then why are you here?" Mimi snapped, her temper rising.

"Mostly 'cause I need the twenty dollars," Baby said in her matter-of-fact tone, "but also 'cause two of my friends is missing, too, kinda like your two friends, and it don't make no kinda sense. Patricia got a baby and she wouldn't leave that little girl for nothin'." Baby shivered in the burning midday heat and scratched herself. It was close on time for her fix. "There's been some talk . . . I ain't paid it much attention till Patricia and Rhonda disappeared . . . they talked a lot about some men who like hurting women."

Mimi felt a rush of recognition. Men who liked hurting women. Shelley and Starry had alluded to but did not specifically articulate the possibility that there existed a gang of men who picked up hookers for sport, not for sex. She hadn't been able to get details because Shelley and Starry were angling for money — big money — despite Mimi's protestations that, unlike some magazines and television programs, her newspaper did not pay for stories. She dug into her pocket and extracted a many-times-folded twenty-dollar bill, which she dropped into Baby's red spandex lap.

"You didn't have to meet me today, so this says, thanks. But get this clear, Baby: I don't pay for information."

"And I don't give away nothin' for free," Baby drawled, getting to her feet and smoothing the four inches of tight red skirt over the minuscule area of her thighs that it covered. She grabbed up her voluminous black bag and slung it over her shoulder and began a deliberate stroll toward the bus stop.

"And by the way, Newspaper Lady, you're fulla shit, you know. No matter what you say, you just paid for information."

The words stung. Mimi stared at Baby's departing form: sequined denim jacket atop red spandex atop black fishnet atop purple patent leather. A hooker who'd just nailed Mimi's equivocating ass right to the Wall of Justification. She exhaled her momentary anger, stood, and caught up with Baby in a few quick strides. They walked together for a block in silence.

"I don't need to be seen with you, Newspaper Lady."

"How can I get in touch with you if I need to?"

"I don't need you gettin' in touch with me, either."

"Two of my friends are missing. Two of your friends are missing. Men are hurting women . . ."

"So what else is new? I gotta go, Newspaper Lady. It's time for my fix."

Once again, Baby's honesty slapped Mimi into a new reality zone. She dug into her back pocket and found a wrinkled card, which she shoved at Baby.

"Then you call me if you need to."

"Why would I ever need you, Newspaper Lady?" Baby drawled, but she took the card and shoved it into the black bag and turned away from Mimi. She took a few steps then turned back. "With a body like you got, Newspaper Lady, you could make a lotta money out here."

Mimi's mouth opened and closed but no words emerged. She knew Baby intended a compliment, but Jesus! Baby laughed at her and in that instant, Mimi realized that Baby was a child, probably not even twenty years old. Her face, unguarded and open in laughter, was lovely.

Baby yelled at Mimi, "You're welcome!" and crossed the street to the corner store that in addition to candy and ice cream and soda pop and cigarettes, also sold coke, smack, and crack. Mimi took her own street-walking-potential body to the gym.

IV

Mimi's nude figure cut a lovely, ghostly image through the candlelit mist, one lost entirely on Gianna who was asleep in the hot tub. They hadn't seen each other for a week, which wasn't unusual given their respective work habits and schedules, and Mimi was slightly put out to find Gianna already in a deeply relaxed, if not comatose, mode. She'd hoped they could see a movie or meet Freddie and Cedric for a drink or catch up with Beverly for a long overdue gossip session. With a sigh, she opened the small refrigerator and took out a bottle of lemon-lime seltzer and thought maybe a quiet night together wouldn't be such a terrible thing. In fact, it was as rare as a night out together, the two of them at the same place, at the same time. They told each other often enough that they worked much too hard and spent not nearly enough time together. Yet, no matter how hard they tried to be together more, the work seemed always to intrude. The obvious solution — that they live together — was no solution for them, not as long as Gianna was a cop and Mimi a reporter. Their work collided constantly — and usually unpleasantly.

Mimi sighed again, releasing the built-up frustration, and surveyed her surroundings with pleasure. Converting the tool shed adjacent to the garage into an oasis of peace and pleasure was one of the smartest things she'd ever done. Even her penny-pinching brother-in-law agreed that it was, in his accountant's jargon, "a wise expenditure of capital." She looked upward and the domed skylight gave her a perfect view of the moon and stars in their velvet vastness. The hothouse plants that filled each of the four corners of the tiny room reached for the light above and spread their boughs into the room. The Italian tile beneath her feet was warm from the steam.

"I hope you don't intend to splash me with cold seltzer just to attract my attention," Gianna said sleepily, eyes still closed.

"I wouldn't dare. And I've heard of x-ray vision, but ears that hear seltzer fizz from the depths of sleep? Amazing." Mimi crossed to her, leaned over the side of the tub, and kissed the top of her head.

Gianna remained unmoving. "I hear all, including your entry."

"So why didn't you say something?"

"I like listening to you think, especially when you don't know I'm listening." Now Gianna opened her eyes and grinned widely at the sight of the naked Mimi. "And I just love your outfit." She opened her arms wide and Mimi stepped into the hot tub, into Gianna's embrace, into the kiss that took up where they'd left off Monday morning at the front door of Gianna's apartment when Mimi departed for work.

"I didn't miss you or anything," Mimi murmured against Gianna's lips.

"I'll fix that," Gianna growled, pulling her into a kiss that kept their mouths and hands busy for quite a little while.

When Mimi could breathe again, she found enough air for a short laugh. "We're going to drown each other in this thing one of these days. We should go to bed."

"I thought you wanted to go out?" Gianna's eyebrows lifted with the inflection in her voice.

Mimi frowned her consternation. "Did you hear me say that?"

"And don't you want to give Freddie a call and see what he and Cedric are up to? We haven't seen them in weeks. And Bev is really pissed that you haven't called her." Gianna's eyes were closed in an unstifled yawn and so missed the look Mimi gave her.

"Mind fuck is what that's called," Mimi muttered darkly.

Gianna laughed the full, rich, throaty laugh that gave Mimi the tingles and then scrutinized her with the wide, clear hazel eyes that made her weak in the knees. "I do love your mind, but it's not your mind I want to —"

Mimi bit the word off her tongue before Gianna could finish, and it was just as well because Gianna immediately began proving her point and they hauled themselves out of the steaming water and skittered, dripping, across the terra cotta tiles and out of the piazza into the garage, through the kitchen, and down the hall to the screened-in porch where Mimi had a futon for sleeping on hot summer nights like this one. And serenaded by crickets and June bugs and alley cats and yard dogs and rap-blasting boom boxes they made love. Until most of the night noises quieted they made love; and, finally, drenched, no longer from hot tub water but from the sweet sweat of sex, they slept. Deeply and fully and gratefully. Until the sun, born hot in the D.C. summer, was well into its west-bound journey, they slept. Until their bodies glistened again with sweat — the sweat of the promise of another 100-degree day, they slept. Until the phone rang.

Gianna mumbled, "Shit!" and then realized that since she wasn't at home the phone couldn't be for her, and she sighed deeply and gratefully, re-buried her face in Mimi's neck, and reclaimed her dream.

When she finally located the phone, Mimi whispered a groggy, "Hello" that turned into a groan when she heard Freddie's recrimination.

"Good thing I didn't hold my breath awaiting your call."

"Oh, God, Freddie. I'm sorry," she whispered into the phone.

"You two planning on getting up some time today?"

"What time is it?"

"Twenty to one."

"In the morning?" Mimi's voice rose above a whisper in pure, amazed indignation. How dare he call her at one in the morning.

"In the afternoon, Miss Thing. What exactly did y'all *do* last night that you need this kind of recovery time?" He was actually laughing out loud and only his standing as her best friend in the world entitled him to mock her and live. She stole a one-eyed glance at the clock to confirm what he'd just told her and slammed her eyes shut in denial of the truth.

"Freddie, I'll call you later, okay?" She hung up without waiting for his response and knew he'd raise hell with her later. She only wanted to sleep. Maybe until one o'clock some afternoon next week.

"What did Freddie say?" Gianna mumbled into her neck.

"That it's one o'clock," Mimi whispered.

"In the morning?" Gianna's voice squeaked on the inflection.

"In the afternoon."

Gianna elbowed Mimi in the ribs and then in the head, she sat up so rapidly and so forcefully. *"One o'clock in the afternoon!"* She jumped out of bed, hair wildly all over her head, hazel eyes wide open in shocked amazement. "I *never* sleep until one o'clock in the afternoon!"

"Never say never. And never get out of bed that

49

fast. I think you just gave me a headache." Mimi, finally awake, rubbed her head where Gianna's elbow had cracked it. She checked the clock again, and the high overhead sun to make sure the clock wasn't lying, and collapsed into the pillow with a great sigh. "And I'm still tired. I could sleep until next week this time. I need a vacation." Mimi closed her eyes and looked as if she would begin her Rip Van Winkle imitation immediately.

Gianna, recovered from the shock, sat on the side of the bed staring at the clock. "When was your last vacation, Mimi?"

"Two years and three months ago." She bolted upright, all her attention focused on Gianna. "And I'm not working on anything right now." She allowed herself to feel the possibility. "Can we get outta here? Even for a week?" She allowed herself to imagine how it would feel to really relax, to slough off the stress and sink deeply into a vegetative state. "A week in Italy," she said dreamily. "Or in France. Maybe somewhere in the Caribbean . . ." She reached for Gianna, pulling her down. "So, can we? Can you take a hate-break, Lieutenant Maglione?"

"Maybe," Gianna mused, snuggling next to her, "though what I had in mind was more like a long weekend in Western Maryland . . ." She struggled to breathe as Mimi smothered her beneath the pillow.

Freddie and Cedric howled with laughter later that night as Mimi repeated the "maybe we'll take a vacation" discussion, especially Freddie, whose cabin in the mountains of Garrett County in Western Maryland was what Gianna had in mind, a place where Mimi had spent so much time that it was more like a second home than her idea of a vacation spot. Mimi and Freddie had been best friends since their UCLA days when, after a few dates, they discovered that not only did they genuinely like each other, but that in matters intimate they both preferred their own gender, and blissfully double-dated with their respective lovers in open secrecy for the duration of their academic sojourn. That they both ended up in D.C. a few years later — Mimi as a star newspaper reporter and Freddie as a star offensive tackle for the Washington Redskins — was nothing short of miraculous.

"Last of the great romantics, huh, Maglione?" Freddie teased Gianna until she blushed, bringing Cedric to her rescue.

"Don't you worry, Luv. I think it's bloody cheeky of them to go on so. After all, it was you who suggested the vac in the first place. Perhaps a bit of appreciation is in order?" Cedric lowered his naturally sexy bass voice another octave and raised his eyebrows at Mimi who missed it because she was rolling on the floor in laughter. Cedric, a poet of some note and a professor of literature at Rutgers, was as tall as six-foot-three-inch Freddie, though with the lithe, lean body of the distance runner instead of the bulk of the football player. He was also Black and British and pronounced his name Cee-Drick. This man's affectation of a Boy George-like cockney and a limp wrist was more than Gianna could handle and she, too, collapsed in laughter.

"Appreciation would be nice," Gianna finally managed, wiping her eyes, "but I'll settle for dinner. I'm starving."

She and Cedric had become close in the year they'd known each other, owing largely to the fact that both were intensely introspective and much more serious-minded than either Mimi or Freddie. In fact, it was only when the four of them were together that Gianna and Cedric loosened up and got silly.

They were at Freddie's place because he had air conditioning and because they hoped that from the vantage point of the terrace of his Georgetown penthouse apartment on the banks of the Potomac River there was the possibility of a breeze. Washington was in the middle of its usual summer heat wave and the temperature at night barely cooled off to seventy-five.

They ate on the terrace with a view of the pleasure boats and cruise liners dotting the Potomac, breeze nowhere to be found. Mimi had made gallons of Sangria, so after a while nobody cared anyway. They ate in peaceful silence, reveling in the joy of their friendship.

"You two really do need a break," Freddie finally said. "I can still feel relaxed when I remember the time Cedric and I spent in Europe last fall."

"Huh," Mimi snorted. "Easy for you to say. You're not married to the workaholic of the Western world. This woman thinks the entire police department will crash and burn if she's not there to keep things going."

"Not fair," Gianna protested. "And besides, I already agreed to maybe taking off a couple of days."

"Oh, great. 'Maybe,' and 'couple of days,' and my

heart should beat fast?" Mimi rolled her eyes at Gianna.

"So, since you can't find your hookers and since you refused to go chasing Nazi skinheads, you really have free time?" Freddie asked Mimi, and the dark protected them all from the absolute stillness that settled over Gianna as the words, "hookers" and "Nazi skinheads" reverberated off her brain walls.

"What hookers can't you find and what Nazi skinheads won't you chase?" Gianna asked carefully, wondering if she'd have to murder Tyler Carson.

"One of the city reporters has a piece in tomorrow's paper about a group of punks uptown terrorizing an old Jewish lady who's a concentration camp survivor. Tyler thinks this group is tied to a bigger group out West somewhere, Idaho or Washington State, and he thought it'd be just nifty if I went out and poked around. It took me a week to convince him that those creeps kill FBI and IRS agents just for sport. Imagine sending a cute little Colored girl to ask them why they act so ugly?"

Mimi was still pissed at the memory of Tyler's insistence that she'd probably be perfectly safe. "Then, a couple of our New York Avenue Ladies of the Evening who'd been stringing me along for months with the promise of a blockbuster of a story disappeared on me. Just vanished into their night-time." Mimi shrugged and poured herself another glass of sangria.

Gianna heard the shattering sound of words and worlds colliding: white supremacists who kill people for sport and prostitutes who vanish into the night. And she felt, once again, her world colliding with Mimi's. If she'd been alone she'd have asked, yelled,

53

out loud, *"Why? Why must she be looking for missing prostitutes and evil-doing skinheads?"*

Grim satisfaction was Gianna's reward on Sunday morning when she read how the newspaper reporter, camped out in her car, caught the skinheads in the act of playing Wagner outside Sophie Gwertzman's house shortly before midnight on the previous Saturday, how the reporter documented their screams to the old woman to visit their tattoo parlor and lampshade factory, how the reporter used the skinheads' own words and deeds to cause them more trouble than the police ever could. But she also read how the reporter concluded that none of these actions, though certainly reprehensible, was illegal; she read how their spokesman, a lawyer, planned to exercise their rights to the letter of the law. And when she turned the page and saw their photographs she went cold inside. These were no scummy punk kids for whom violence was a substitute for discipline and direction. These were grown men in whom the evil was deliberate and directed and Gianna knew with a wrenching certainty that she had not seen the last of them.

Mimi answered the phone, her mind on the immigration report she was reading, so the drugged, guttural voice registered no recognition in her consciousness.

"Is that you, Newspaper Lady?"

"Excuse me? Who is this?"

"It's me, Baby Doll. You know them two girls you was lookin' for? Well, you can stop lookin' 'cause they dead."

Mimi instantly forgot about illegal immigrants and plunged right into the meaning of Baby Doll's slurred words. It occurred to her that Baby Doll was in need of a fix and angling for money; but she also felt strongly that the girl was telling the truth. Mimi always attributed her success as an investigative reporter to the thing in her brain that categorized words as they came to her ears from others' mouths: there were True Words; there were Lies; and there was Bullshit, which was usually a combination of truth and lies deliberately designed to obfuscate. Baby Doll's words were true.

"Do you know what happened to them, Baby?"

"Oh, I heard some things," Baby intoned much too casually.

"Some things like what?" Mimi tensed because she knew what was coming next.

"That'll cost you, Newspaper Lady."

"I told you that I don't pay for information."

"And I told you you were fulla shit. You wanna know what I know, Newspaper Lady, meet me at the Connecticut Avenue Diner at two-thirty."

"Why the hurry?" Mimi looked at the row of clocks on the wall and saw that she'd need to leave now to be on time.

" 'Cause I'm hungry and 'cause I need a fix, that's why," Baby said, irritated but with the guilelessness that never ceased to impress Mimi.

"Baby, I hate drugs."

"Then don't take 'em. And you can either meet

me and pay me or don't meet me and don't pay me but don't lecture me 'cause I don't want to hear it." And with that, Mimi was left listening to the dial tone and cursing drugs as the greatest evil ever constructed by man.

Someplace like the Connecticut Avenue Diner probably existed in some form in every big city in America, Mimi thought. An old place, spruced up and modernized, but eternally old. New booths of bright red pseudo-leather and lots of silver-looking chrome probably intended to suggest that it was polished on a regular basis. New miniature juke boxes at each booth with vintage country, blues, and rock 'n roll tunes. The new neon sign blinking continuously outside and reflecting its red and green glow back into the not quite clean windows. A waitress who hasn't seen her twenty-fifth birthday, and a short order cook who probably couldn't remember his sixty-fifth but knew all the regular customers not only by name but how long they'd been customers because he'd been there thirty-two years himself. Laminated and therefore non-greasy menus spoke of eggs and omelettes of every kind and description, accompanied by sausage and bacon and ham and grits and potatoes and all with or without cheese, all of the above to be had with cholesterol-free quasi-eggs and whole wheat or raisin toast instead of old-fashioned white bread. Pancakes, waffles, French toast served twenty-four hours a day. Smoking, drinking and bad attitudes not permitted. One sign above the cash register read, *In God we trust. All others pay cash.* The other read, *If you're in a hurry you're in the wrong place.*

Mimi knew that people came to the Connecticut Avenue Diner to eat and to read their newspapers — racing forms, sports pages, help wanted sections, advice columns; to argue politics; to work the kinks out of troubled relationships; to drink better coffee than was available at home; to be catered to and ignored at the same time. Men and women in the business suits of the commercial end of Connecticut Avenue shared booths and counter stools with beauticians, taxi drivers, construction workers, kids cutting class, hookers meeting reporters. The Connecticut Avenue Diner was the kind of place that had seen every kind of person and heard every kind of story and no matter how new and shiny the fixtures, the building had been in the same spot since 1937 and that much life raised the cholesterol count whether or not you ate the food.

Mimi opened the door, spied a couple standing up to leave in the far left corner, and sprinted for the booth just as a guy in paint-spattered khakis came out of the bathroom and aimed toward it. Mimi slid into the seat, beating him by a hair of a second. He scowled at her and plopped onto a stool at the counter next to a teen-aged girl with orange spiky hair who held up a bottle of ketchup, waiting, in inane imitation of a commercial, for the stuff to come out. Mimi didn't need to read the menu to know that she couldn't safely eat anything listed, but she studied it anyway to have something to do while she waited for Baby Doll. Waited and decided how to say what she knew she must say without having Baby Doll explode.

The stillness that enveloped the room was Mimi's notice that Baby Doll had arrived, and she was surprised at how angry she felt at the hypocrisy of the people in the crowded and now silent diner. She had no qualms about believing that fully half of the men in the place had paid for the services of a prostitute at some time in their lives. And too many women allowed themselves to be treated worse than hookers for them to look down their noses at a woman because she sold her body. But as Mimi turned toward the door, she had to admit that Baby's appearance was sufficient to quiet even the sizzling bacon and burgers on the grill. Baby's wig was peroxide white and cascaded at least a full twenty inches down her back. She wore thigh-high white patent leather boots with red laces and a skin-tight white leotard that began in the vicinity of her crotch and ended at the tops of her breasts. Underneath she wore a sheer red body stocking. On her nose perched a pair of wire-rimmed sunglasses with yellow tinted lenses, over which she peered in search of Mimi.

"Hey Sister! You can't hustle in here!" the short order cook yelled over the noise of sizzling grease.

"It's a diner, Sugah, not a motel. I got that much figured out," Baby called back without the slightest trace of rancor. And she grinned good-naturedly at the people she passed en route to the booth where Mimi sat. The girl with the ketchup smiled back and the two boys in the booth next to Mimi gave her the thumbs up.

"Hey, Newspaper Lady. What's up?" Baby slid into the booth across from Mimi.

"The temperature. Hot as hell out there."

"That's why I said meet me in here. I'm hungry. You hungry?" Baby picked up the menu, scanned it with a practiced, nonchalant air, slapped it shut, and looked around for the waitress.

"No, I'm not hungry. Listen, Baby..." Mimi was cut off as the waitress sidled up to the table with a closed-lidded glance at Baby, who totally ignored the dirty look and didn't wait to be asked her order.

"I want waffles and sausage. And some scrambled eggs. Sure you ain't hungry?" she asked Mimi.

"Coffee, black," Mimi said so that the waitress would go away.

"That how you keep that body? Ain't healthy, you know."

Mimi was irritated and didn't mind showing it. "I don't eat this kind of food. I'm a vegetarian. Now can we get to the business at hand?" She was edgy because she knew she was about to disappoint Baby and she wanted to get on with it.

"My friend Patricia was one of those. Vegetarian. One of the other girls, too. Said they liked eating that funny food. Not me. Personally, I can't eat —"

"One of what girls?" Mimi's spine tingled.

"One of your friends, that Shelley Kelley. I heard she was really into that whole spiritual thing. Don't you get bored just eating vegetables?"

Part of Mimi's brain urged her to regain control of the situation, while the other part admitted that this was Baby's show all the way. She knew that Baby regarded her on-demand presence as tacit agreement to pay for information. She also knew that she had no intention of giving Baby money, so that it was cruel to lead her on. Yet... and yet...

"Baby, can you slow down and tell me in as few words as possible about this 'spiritual thing' so we can talk about what we're here to talk about?"

"Ain't you a demanding bitch?" Baby intoned, and with a shrug, explained that members of what sounded to Mimi like an Ashram or some other communal group had begun working among the street prostitutes, urging them to take precautions against AIDS, offering free vegetarian meals at their head-quarters uptown, and offering to teach yoga and meditation as a path to salvation. Free food was the initial attraction, according to Baby, though in the case of her friend, Patricia, the spiritual aspect had taken hold quickly and strongly.

"She started talkin' a lot about findin' peace and joy inside herself, and about forgiveness. Stuff like that. And I guess it must've worked 'cause she got clean . . ." For the briefest instant Baby was overcome by a palpable sadness. Then she shook it off, resumed her usual languor, and remembered why she was inhaling waffles, sausage and eggs at the Connecticut Avenue Diner. "And that's enough free information, Newspaper Lady. Where's my money?"

"I don't pay for information and I don't pay for drugs."

An ugly look crossed Baby's face, anger tinged with desperation and need. The need for drugs. "Don't fuck with me," she said quietly.

"I'm not. I'll help you if I can, Baby, pay your rent or your phone bill, but I won't buy your drugs or give you money to buy drugs."

Their eyes met and held and Baby slowly stood, gathered her belongings, turned and walked away without another word or a backward glance.

Mimi felt let down. Not because she'd not gotten all the information possible from Baby: she'd expected that result when she made the decision not to pay her. But she'd also expected ballistics. Histrionics. She'd expected Baby to yell and scream and curse and be angry. That would have made her feel better, would have justified her decision. Now she felt manipulative and dishonest. Because she'd gotten information from Baby after all, a lead about some group who proselytized in the streets among the hookers, and though she'd thoroughly check it out, it didn't make sense that people who preached internal joy, provided free vegetarian meals, and taught yoga and meditation to prostitutes, would then systematically murder them. But then, lots of things didn't make sense to her. It didn't make sense that teenagers sold their bodies for drugs and money. It didn't make sense that the drugs were so easily and readily available. It didn't make sense that she found herself caring what the hell Marlene Somebody aka Baby Doll did with her life. It didn't make sense that she really wanted to know what had happened to those other girls, not for a newspaper article but because some part of her believed that whatever happened to them was unwarranted. It didn't make sense that it was a hundred fucking degrees for the fifth day in a row and it was only June. July and August would be hell.

Tim McCreedy somehow managed to create the illusion that he had contorted and compressed his weightlifter's body into that of a mincing, nerdy twerp, as he demonstrated for the Hate Crimes team his queenly badgering of one of the investigators in Homicide. He played to his colleagues gathered in the Think Tank as if to the Saturday night crowd at the Comedy Club.

"By the time I finished talking to Mr. Boy about the sanctity of the evidence chain, he was ready to throw a knife in *my* heart. And your Captain Pelligrino, Lieutenant. So very embarrassed to have to admit that portions of the files were missing. Until I found them. 'How the hell did you know where to look,' Mr. Boy growled at me when the Captain left the room. 'Simple,' I told him. 'I just have to pretend to be as brilliant as you and everything just falls into place.' If looks could kill, I'd be one dead queen."

Lynda Lopez was laughing so hard Bobby Gilliam had to slap her on the back to restore her breath. Eric, tears in his eyes, gave up trying to maintain decorum. Kenny Chang stood and tried to imitate Tim's mannerisms. Cassie Ali let out a whoop then hurled herself at Tim and wrapped him in a bear hug that almost shut off his breath, quite an accomplishment since he was a foot taller and almost a hundred pounds heavier than she.

"McCreedy, you're beautiful," she intoned in her deadpan voice. "May we always fight on the same side, and may we always win." She raised an imaginary glass in an imaginary toast and they all joined in saluting McCreedy.

"Good work, Tim," Gianna said through her laughter.

"Thanks, Lieutenant," he said, always knowing

when to cut off the act. "I hope none of this comes back to haunt you."

"They better hope it doesn't come back to haunt them," Kenny snorted from his Tim-like pose. "They're the ones who screwed up the files, not us."

And Tim McCreedy had unscrewed them. He had located the misplaced autopsy and forensic reports; the missing death certificate; the witness and interview lists. It had taken three tedious weeks. Then he had spent another week helping Cassie construct her file on Andrea Thomas, aka Starry Knight; helping Lynda construct her file on Sandra King, aka Shelley Kelley; helping Bobby construct his file on Rhonda Green, aka Lady Day; helping Kenny construct his file on Patricia McIntyre, aka Patty Mack. That was after he'd confirmed his boss's fears and suspicions and privately delivered to her the two additional files: There were at least two more victims of the knife-wielding killer, Jane Does, never identified and therefore never claimed. Pieces of these Jane Doe files had been merged with the other files — not intentionally, Tim had emphasized — but no less disconcertingly. In one case, the knife had been removed from the victim's chest before authorities took possession of the body — in other words, Tim had told Gianna, somebody stole the knife from the murdered woman's body while it lay in an alley — and it was months before investigators realized that the murdered woman probably was a Daniel Boone victim, though without the weapon, they'd never know for sure.

* * * * *

The Chief of Police didn't walk so much as propel himself forward on the balls of his feet, bouncing a bit with each step, generating urgency and immediacy and a sense of purpose. He was pacing back and forth in his huge office on the top floor of the Municipal Center, his shiny black shoes sinking with every step almost to invisibility in the plush gold carpet. When he'd sent for her, told her to be in his office at seven-thirty, she'd thought he wanted an update on the Daniel Boone investigation, so she gave him an update. Walked him through every detail of each of the cases. Talked to him like the homicide detective he once was.

Now, watching him, she wasn't certain what he wanted. He'd ceased his pacing. When in repose, he stood almost on tiptoe, heels raised slightly off the floor, torso leaning forward, ready to launch into action at the slightest provocation. He was fifty-four years old and it was only the grey in his hair and moustache and the network of fine lines around his eyes and mouth that verified that truth, for he could, on any day, step into the ring and become again the Golden Gloves boxer whose card name thirty-odd years ago was Scrappy. He was, to her dismay, in exactly that frame of mind.

"Don't complain to me about the sorry state of some files, Maglione. Don't you read the newspapers? You're lucky there *were* files." He thrust his hands into his pockets and jingled the change in one of them.

The gesture, for some reason, irritated her more than his words. She didn't need the newspapers to tell her that D.C. had one of the highest murder rates in the country, and one of the lowest case closure rates. She didn't need the papers to tell her what she read from the sag in Vince Pelligrino's shoulders. But she did need the Chief to respond to her concerns, especially since he'd ordered her to report to him and not to her immediate boss, a situation that made her increasingly uneasy.

"Anyway," he continued in his rapid-fire delivery, "you suspected all along that what we saw was just the tip of the iceberg. Now you know you were right."

"Is that supposed to make me feel better?" She was getting angry and did nothing to disguise the fact. "You want me to break my arm patting myself on the back, or do you want me determine just how serious a problem we have?"

"I know how serious the problem is, Maglione," he snapped at her. "And I'm gonna tell you how serious it is. Serious enough for me to move Hate Crimes into my office." He dropped that bomb and stood on his toes waiting for it to register, waiting for her to grasp the full impact.

"Have I done something wrong?" She was so angry she barely spoke above a whisper and she had to fight to get the words out.

"You do everything right, Maglione. Too right sometimes, and that can be a problem, especially in an election year —"

"I never would have believed that you, of all people, would let politics dictate your decisions." She was drained of anger, but could not have named all the emotions she felt, though confusion would have been near the top of the list.

"The mayor will have a hard enough time getting re-elected without the Daniel Boone killings, and I can't keep a lid on it if Eddie Davis is talking about it at report every week." He was talking even faster than usual, the words tumbling from his mouth like shells from an automatic weapon. "I want this case worked, Maglione, but I want it worked off the books."

"So now we're cowboy cops?" She used the department slang for those specialty units that reported directly to the Office of the Chief. She knew of three such units: immigration, drugs, and gang and violence task forces. It was rumored that there were others but since they answered only to the Chief, only he knew for sure. The up side to being a cowboy unit was that she'd have access to every conceivable resource — manpower and hardware and budget. The down side was that the specialty task forces were resented by the regular units that had to get by with not enough of anything.

"Does Inspector Davis know?" She realized in that instant how much she would miss Davis, and she was sorry for what, she knew, would be perceived as some failure on his part. Politics begets more of the same, and since politics dictated the Chief's action, politics would govern the speculation about the reasons for it, and Inspector Eddie Davis would be perceived the loser and she would be perceived the winner, since cowboy cops were perceived as the elite.

"He knows," the Chief said briefly, and she knew that it had not been a pleasant conversation.

She tried to think of something to say but could not. He had, it seemed, altered the nature of their twenty-year relationship in a matter of moments. She was almost tempted to salute him. As she was

66

imagining how he'd react to that, he took her off the hook.

"What are you doing about the goddamn Nazis? I sure as hell don't want anything to happen to that old lady."

"I planted the newspaper story."

"Good for you, Maglione!" A wide grin cracked his face and he seemed to raise several inches on his toes. "That's how the game's played. You're learning."

"I thought so, Chief. I thought so." And she left to go consider life as a cowboy cop, stopping on the way to see if Inspector Davis was still in his office, relieved to find that he was not, because she didn't know what to say to him. So much had changed in so brief a time.

She walked the three flights down to her own office because she didn't want to encounter anyone in the elevator. And when she opened her door, she was almost surprised to find that things were still the same as she'd left them. The familiarity of the place restored some of her equilibrium. She took off her jacket and draped it neatly on the hanger behind the door. She crossed to her desk, dropped heavily into the chair and sighed loudly.

Her thoughts were all over the place so she switched on the computer and called up the statistical analysis she was preparing. Maybe if she could work she could quiet the doubts that were buzzing about her like a swarm of angry hornets. A great lump of uneasiness lay heavily within her and she struggled to define it. It was more than disappointment in the Chief's politicization of her mission. She didn't like politics but she understood that she lived in a political world and she accepted that. The Chief was a political appointee and so, by extension, was she. When she objectively viewed the benefits of heading up a cowboy unit, it could only make her look good, especially if she made a collar. So what was the source of the sick feeling in her gut?

She looked from the ringing phone, to the clock that told her it was nine o'clock, and back to the phone, and wondered if she had a date with Mimi that she'd forgotten. Otherwise, who the hell could be calling her at work so late? She picked up the phone.

"Lieutenant Maglione."

"This is Tyler Carson, Lieutenant. Sorry to bother you."

"No bother, Mr. Carson, though I should think you'd have better things to do with your time."

"Better than spending most of the waking hours of the most productive years of my life working fourteen-hour days? Whatever would make you think that, Lieutenant."

She laughed out loud. She'd only met him once, but she remembered that Mimi described him as alternating between boringly normal and normally boring. His saving grace, according to Mimi, was that he was the best editor in the business.

"Thanks for the levity, Mr. Carson. I needed that. What can I do for you?"

"You can tell me whether you sicced the B-MOG on the Nazis 'cause if you did, you have my heightened respect and my undying gratitude. It's a hell of a good story."

Gianna was rendered speechless, and it took so long for his words to take the shape of rational thought in her brain that he misunderstood her silence.

"Ah, listen, Lieutenant . . . ah, I'm sorry if I . . ."

"Did I do *what*?" She almost raised her voice at him.

He hurriedly explained that he'd just received an irate and almost threatening phone call from the attorney for the neo-Nazi group that paid nocturnal visits to Sophie Gwertzman, complaining that his clients — the guys playing concentration camp music outside the old woman's house — had just had their Constitutional rights violated by members of the B-MOG.

"The B-MOG." She made it a statement, not a question, but he responded as if it had been.

"The Black Men On Guard, the guys who wear black jeans, black T-shirts, black combat boots and control access and entry to —"

"I know *who* they are. They did *what*?"

"They caused the Nazis to tuck tail and run."

"This early in the evening? I thought they only played their dirty tricks in the wee hours of the morning."

"They've been varying their times since we did the story, and keeping well within the noise ordinance. Did you see it, by the way? The story?"

"I saw it, and I expected some kind of fallout, but not this. Not this." She had anticipated that the Nazi group would respond or retaliate in some way to the newspaper article, but she had not expected that another powerful and potentially dangerous organization would join the fray. "What exactly did they do? The MOGgers, I mean?"

"It is my understanding that there were about ten of them. They surrounded the Nazis' truck and

69

ordered them to turn off the music, to leave the neighborhood, and not to return. When the Nazis did not obey, the MOGgers picked up their truck —"

"I beg your pardon?" Gianna felt lightheaded.

"You heard correctly. They picked up the truck — one of those little Toyota short beds as I understand it — and began to carry it down the street. At which point the Nazis agreed to leave voluntarily."

"Are they still there? The MOGgers, I mean?"

"I've got a reporter on the way to the scene. I'll let you know." He hesitated for a brief moment. "Lieutenant?"

"Mr. Carson, you've just told me everything I know about this situation," she answered his question before he asked. *But I intend to find out a lot more,* she told herself as she thanked him and hung up the phone with one hand and reached across her desk for the Rolodex with the other.

Black Men On Guard was not unknown to the Hate Crimes Unit. There were those who believed it to be an organization that preached hate and advocated violence, much like the Nazis. As the result of an investigation two years ago, Gianna had learned quite a bit about the MOGgers, and had developed a cordial and mutually respectful relationship with Yusuf Shakur, the forty-eight-year-old head of the Southeast D.C.-based organization. A soft-spoken, humorous man, he always delighted in the fact that strangers and outsiders found that once they knew him, they actually liked him, for his exterior demeanor and his past reputation would suggest otherwise. Shakur was a large, powerfully built, ominous-looking man who, in the early 1960s, was a devout follower of Malcolm X and the Nation of Islam and then, after the Muslim leader's assassination, a vociferous member of the Black Panther Party. Like many Panthers and Muslims, Shakur had spent time in prison, and rather than seek to conceal this fact of his past, he wore it like a badge of honor: it validated him in the eyes of the young men he recruited for his organization. And Yusuf Shakur had never retracted the twenty-five-year-old pro-violence and anti-Semitic statements he had made as a young firebrand, statements that placed his name in the company of the well-known activists of the day.

Shakur had organized Black Men On Guard in the mid-1980s specifically to reclaim Washington's inner city neighborhoods from drug dealers and users. From the densely populated housing projects of Southeast D.C., across the Anacostia River, B-MOG, as it quickly became known, grew and spread so that Yusuf Shakur now headed an organization that touched every neighborhood in every part of the city, and that was lauded and funded by churches and civic groups and, finally, grudgingly accepted by politicians for accomplishing what the police had been unable to: wherever members of B-MOG positioned themselves, drug dealers had no wish to be, for MOGgers did not hesitate to use threats of violence, and actual violence when threats failed, to convince gang members and dealers to vacate turf MOGgers claimed as theirs. But there could be no disputing the enmity that continued to exist between MOGgers, many of whom were Muslims, and Jews. So why, she asked Shakur now, were Black Men On Guard tonight guarding the home of an old Jewish woman?

"It's not unusual, Lieutenant. The presence of B-MOG is frequently a deterrent to crime."

"Yes, I know. But let's face it, we're not talking about drug dealers and gang-bangers here."

"I know that, Lieutenant," he replied with a touch of pique. "We're dealing with the only kind of scum that could be lower than dealers and bangers. Besides, we never refuse a request for help from citizens."

"Are you telling me that you were specifically invited to Sophie Gwertzman's house?"

"How and why else would we know to be there?"

"Does it bother you that the woman you're protecting is Jewish?"

"It bothers me, Lieutenant, that the woman is the helpless victim of vicious cowards for the second time in her life." His voice had become tight and cold.

Gianna could hear that Shakur was losing patience with her but she had just one more question to which she was certain she knew the answer but which she had to ask. "Mr. Shakur, are you acquainted with Cassandra Ali?"

"But of course, Lieutenant. I'd have thought that much was obvious," Shakur said with a deep laugh.

She hung up, swiveled around in her chair to face the window, and looked down on a deserted Judiciary Square. It looked sad, lonely, and a bit shabby without the many hundreds of people — cops and criminals, judges and lawyers, secretaries, clerks, reporters, jurors, crime victims, the curious — who daily gave meaning to the cluster of buildings that constituted the square: The police department, the old and new Superior Court buildings, the Public Defenders' and U.S. Attorneys' buildings. She was one of those people, part of the thing called the Criminal Justice System. She was one of the good guys. Or once was. Now she was a cowboy. And she realized suddenly, acutely, what she didn't like about the situation: she was completely vulnerable. Out on a limb without benefit of a safety net. Inspector Davis would no longer approve or disapprove of her plans and actions. There was nobody to check in with or answer to. If she got lucky and broke the case, good for her. If she didn't, she shouldered the blame alone. Not that she minded carrying her own weight. But she did mind not having the advantage of Eddie Davis's experience and insight. She'd like, for example, to hear his views on Black Men On Guard protecting an elderly Jewish woman from a bunch of neo-Nazis. It was one of the most improbable scenarios she could imagine. And Tyler Carson was right. It would make one hell of a good story.

V

Mimi was ambivalent about the virtues of sidewalk cafes. Or, more accurately, she was ambivalent about the virtues of sidewalk cafes in places like New York and Washington. A boulangerie in Paris or a trattoria in Rome were one thing. The feast for her eyes and her spirit was worth whatever amount of carbon monoxide she might ingest with her *vin rouge* or *bruscetta e mozzarella*. Granted, carbon monoxide was just as deadly in the French, Italian or English language, but she flat out refused to eat outside in New York City, and she wasn't thrilled about it at DuPont Circle in Washington. But she was here anyway, waiting for Beverly and, later, for Gianna and for Sylvia, Bev's most recent heart interest.

She'd be happy to see Bev. They were rebuilding their friendship after a stormy breakup two years ago that had left Bev all but unable to be anything more than barely polite to Mimi. And when Mimi had finally moved her ego far enough out of the way to see the truth, she'd had to admit that Beverly's anger was justified. Mimi had been a disaster as a lover, but she loved Beverly deeply, and wanted her friendship. It had helped that Gianna and Beverly were becoming good friends at the same time that Gianna and Mimi were becoming lovers. Gianna was the bridge they needed, the impartial and nonjudgmental arbiter. At the time, Gianna didn't know either of them well enough to have an opinion about who'd done what to whom, so she either steered clear of them altogether when there was tension, or she pushed and prodded until one or the other relinquished stubbornness. Now Mimi and Bev were close enough again that Bev had something really important to share with her. So, here Mimi was, breathing fumes and sweating on Seventeenth Street.

Fortunately, there'd been a break in the monster heat wave and for the end of July it was actually quite pleasant at about eighty degrees. She'd arrived a little early because she'd forgone her usual Saturday morning run through Rock Creek Park and instead cut her grass and washed her car and made her weekly calls to her relatives in California. She'd learned years ago that the best way not to spend an hour on the telephone with her Aunt Louise was to call her before she'd had her second cup of coffee. Eleven a.m. in D.C. was eight a.m. in L.A. and Aunt Lou was finishing her first cup of coffee. She'd pass the phone to Uncle Walter, who hated talking on the phone. He always asked how she was, how Freddie was, whether they were married yet, how her job was, and said good-bye. Aunt Flo and Uncle Jimmy were always en route to the tennis court, so that conversation was always brief. Her cousin Amanda was always asleep and always reminded her of the three-hour time difference. Her cousin Jeff was never at home so she always left a message on his machine. She was smugly satisfied when she made her final call of the morning, to her father.

She looked up from reading the menu to see Beverly walking toward her. The woman, quite simply, was stunning. She wore a white skirt of some clingy fabric that seemed delighted to be wrapped around her hips and legs, and a white sleeveless T-shirt. She was the color of dark chocolate with hints of bronze, long dreadlocks held in place by one of the many pieces of African print material she kept for that purpose. She was long and lean (except for a generous endowment of bust and hip) and walked with her head in the sky and Mimi felt the same reaction as the first time she saw her: what an incredible woman!

They embraced and Mimi held her for a long moment, hoping Bev felt the love she couldn't find the words to express.

"You just get more beautiful," Mimi said when they'd seated themselves.

"Just what I was thinking about you," Bev said with a grin. "Looks like Gianna agrees with you."

"No, actually, I agree with her. Or else." Bev laughed at the joke and Mimi knew they'd cleared a major hurdle. Relief settled around them warm as the humidity of the summer afternoon air, and they ordered salsa and chips and Dos Equis.

"So what is it you want to tell me?" Mimi prodded. "You sounded so excited on the phone. Could it be love?" she teased.

"Could be," Bev said with a shadow of a smile, "but that's not what I want to tell you." She reached into the brightly colored string bag she'd hung on the back of her chair and extracted a pamphlet, which she offered to Mimi.

"Midtown Psychotherapy Associates," Mimi read out loud in a puzzled tone. "Referrals accepted from Educational, Juvenile Justice, and Social Service agencies." Mimi's look of puzzlement grew. "Bev, I don't —"

"Well, open it, silly thing, and read the inside."

Mimi scowled but did as ordered, continuing to read out loud: "Individual, group and family counseling . . . blah, blah, blah . . . Joyce Gray, M.D . . . Eugene Cooper, Ph.D . . . *Beverly Connors, Licensed Clinical Social Worker!*" Mimi finished with a whoop. "Now will you explain?" she asked with mock patience.

"I'm leaving the school system. To be more precise, I've left. For the first time in my life, I won't be going back to school in the fall."

Mimi was shocked and her mouth literally hung open. Beverly laughed at her.

"Close your mouth. You look moronic."

"You love working with those children!"

"I can't do it any more, Mimi. Not the way it is

now. I could handle poverty and ignorance and even lack of parental interest. And I managed to deal with the drugs. But the violence. I can't handle the violence. Four teachers were assaulted last year, Mimi, one by a nine-year-old. We've had guns and knives confiscated, along with vials of crack and cocaine. We now have new guidelines about how to touch children —"

"What the hell does that mean?" Mimi didn't know where to direct the anger she was feeling, so she growled at Bev.

"Exactly what I said." Bev continued in a cold, brittle tone that sounded as if she were reading from an instruction manual. "We can no longer hold and comfort them for fear of being accused of abuse if we touch them the wrong way, or if the child believes we did. We can no longer tend their wounds if they bloody themselves playing or fighting for fear of AIDS. If I think a child is being physically abused, I can call Social Services and have the child placed in their care immediately, but not if I suspect sexual abuse." Bev's shoulders sagged in sadness and all Mimi's anger drained away.

She reached across the table and took both her hands. "I apologize, Bev, for not knowing these things. For not being there for you while you coped with this madness. This must be awful for you."

"Awful would be easy to bear," she said simply.

And they sat with their feelings for a moment. Mimi took up the pamphlet again, reading it silently this time. "Jesus, that's a tough neighborhood," she said finally. "If you were going to leave, you should have left."

"I'm not running away from the fight, Mimi. I'm

just choosing a different weapon. Same battleground, same enemy, different weapon. I think I can accomplish more in a clinic setting than I ever could in the school system. The rules too often get in the way of results."

"I think you're right. The more I observe systems, the more convinced I am that they're designed to fail. The inherent stupidity is overwhelming sometimes."

Bev looked at her skeptically. "Has Gianna ever heard you say those words?"

Mimi laughed. "Oh, she knows my innermost feelings about the workings of the criminal justice system, including her very own police department."

"Must make for interesting dinner conversation," Bev said wryly.

"Actually, it doesn't," Mimi said quietly.

Bev looked at her closely. "You can't mean you two don't talk about standing on different sides of the same fence?" When Mimi didn't respond, Bev looked hesitant but allowed herself a final word. "What you two do is too intense not to share it with each other. Now. I'm butting out."

Mimi was about to tell her it was okay, that she probably needed to discuss it with somebody, when Bev's face changed and Mimi felt an instant of sharp jealousy because that look was the look of love. She turned to see what Bev saw and the jealousy pang got sharper. This was, no doubt, Sylvia.

She was taller than Mimi by a couple of inches and walked with a loose, easy stride. The baggy britches and long shirt could not disguise the fact that a perfect body lived within. Her hair resembled Mimi's in that there was a lot of it and it existed in defiance of any particular style. Mimi called her own "free hair." Sylvia's attitude seemed to suggest that she didn't need to call hers anything. She kissed Beverly and greeted Mimi warmly and sat down in what seemed like one fluid motion. Mimi had never seen a more relaxed, at ease, and at the same time more totally in control person. Sylvia caught the waitress's eye and raised three fingers, ordering fresh, cold beers for them. Sylvia's entire arrival couldn't have taken more than half a minute, and Bev's eyes never left her. Yep, Mimi thought. Definitely love.

They spent the next few moments getting acquainted and waiting for the beers, moments during which Mimi learned that Sylvia, an Ohio native and former professional dancer, taught dance and yoga at her own studio. Gianna arrived at the same time as the beers and while they were waiting for the waitress to bring another and for more salsa and chips, she apologized for being late by explaining that she had just been the victim of an attempted street mugging at the cash withdrawal machine outside her bank.

"Poor guy," she said as she concluded her story. "He just picked the wrong person to stick up."

"Poor guy my ass!" Mimi snorted. "He'd probably have shot you if you hadn't been trained to kick him in the balls. And besides, how many times have I asked you not to use the machine on that deserted side street?"

Gianna ignored Mimi's chastisement. "The gun wasn't real and he was no criminal. He was a scared, broke kid from a farm in South Carolina who needed money for food," Gianna said wearily, but with no trace of anger.

"So he thought it was okay to put a gun in your face and steal your money?" Bev's impatience was evident. "That's crap, Gianna, and believe me when I tell you that fear doesn't care whether or not a gun is real. I know from experience."

"You didn't tell me that part," Mimi said accusingly.

"That part doesn't matter, Mimi. What matters is that we've got to stop finding reasons to excuse and accept violent behavior."

"Just don't suggest that we lock them all up and throw away the key," Gianna said. "Even if I wanted to, which I don't, and even if I could, which I can't, there is absolutely no reason to believe that such action has any preventive effect at all."

"But if punishment isn't a deterrent," Sylvia posed, "what is?"

"Yeah, somebody tell me so I can have the exclusive on the story of the century. I could use a Pulitzer." Mimi almost succeed in keeping the cynicism out of her voice.

Beverly laughed and began to say something but stopped, her eyes focused on something behind Mimi, who turned to find herself face to face with Baby Doll.

"Hey Newspaper Lady."

Because she was watching Baby, Mimi could only imagine the startled looks she got from Gianna, Bev and Sylvia when she said, "Hi, Baby. How are you? I almost didn't recognize you."

Baby had on baggy jeans and a man-sized pullover, sneakers, and wore her hair in a short natural cut. Without the wig and the costume of her profession, she looked like the child she was, though the long sleeves in the eighty-degree heat gave her away as a junkie.

"You think I dress like that all the time? I ain't crazy, you know. And even people like me gotta take a day off sometimes."

Mimi was at a loss for words. Baby was not.

"Her manners ain't so good, I guess. My name is Marlene," she said, shaking hands around the table. Bev was amused, Gianna was bemused, having accurately assessed both Baby's profession and her addiction, and Sylvia couldn't quite believe it was happening. Mimi took one look at their faces and recovered her equilibrium.

"Baby . . . ah . . . Marlene and I almost worked a story together."

"Yeah, almost. Till you blew it, Newspaper Lady. But you know where to find me if you change your mind." And with that, Baby tossed a wave to the table and continued her amble down the street.

Mimi had no choice but to explain, which she did in the broadest possible terms. Bev thought it a shame that someone as pretty and as obviously smart as Baby was living so wasted a life. Sylvia didn't realize that reporters really did consort with prostitutes and drug dealers and gang members — she'd thought that was all television hype, and Mimi rushed to assure her that most of it was. But it was Gianna's reaction that put Mimi on notice, for she reacted virtually not at all. She just sat there with that bemused look on her face, and Mimi knew it meant that she was working the prostitution murders as an active case.

Goddammit! Here we go again, Mimi thought as she remembered the last time they both had chased the same story and how it almost ended their relationship before it began.

VI

If Sylvia was surprised to see Mimi outside her studio six days later, she gave no hint. She received Mimi warmly and invited her back to an interior garden and offered ice-cold lemonade. Mimi was impressed that Sylvia owned the building and had a dance and yoga enrollment schedule that kept her and another instructor busy five days a week. The more Mimi learned of Sylvia the more she liked her. She was better for Bev than Mimi ever had been and Mimi was happy for both of them. She told Sylvia as much, then told her why she was there.

"So there *was* more to the Baby Doll story than met the ear," Sylvia said with a laugh. But she turned immediately serious when she put her mind to the task at hand. "There are quite a few spiritual communities in the city and suburbs that do some kind of outreach, Mimi, and any one of them could be what you're looking for."

"I didn't know they went in for that kind of thing. I thought missionary work was more the purview of Western Christianity and not Eastern mysticism."

"It's not that cut and dried," Sylvia said slowly. "It's not as simple as East versus West, fundamentalism versus mysticism."

"What is it, then?" Mimi asked, genuinely curious.

"A lot of it, very simply, is about restoring the balance." Sylvia smiled at the look on Mimi's face, and continued. "That means trying to get us human animals back in tune with nature and our other relations. See, we're the ones out of whack. We're the ones that disturbed the balance in the first place —"

"Yeah, I know that and you know that but what does that have to do with proselytizing among prostitutes?" Mimi's curiosity had turned to skepticism.

"You said Baby said AIDS prevention was the purpose of the outreach?" When Mimi nodded Sylvia raised her palms and shrugged. "And what could be more representative of the destruction of the balance than AIDS? I don't even know anymore how many of my friends have been taken. Do you? Do you still count?"

"No," Mimi said quietly. "I don't. I count the ones who are still here."

"Exactly. And that's how we restore the balance. We correct the error as we find it."

"And hookers are the error?" Mimi raised her eyebrows.

"Certainly not," Sylvia said vehemently. "They're the victims of the error."

"And victims," Mimi said slowly, understanding dawning, "are a logical place to sow seeds of correction."

"You'd make a great wooly-headed mystic, Mimi," Sylvia said with a laugh.

"Thanks, Oh great Swami," Mimi said, sharing the laughter. "Do you think you can find out who's working with the hook . . . ah the prostitutes?"

"I'll find them. And when I find them, I think I'll join them. They're doing a good thing. Besides," Sylvia said with a grin, "I like your friend, Baby Doll. She's worth the effort."

They passed one of the studios on the way to the front door and Mimi stopped to watch a yoga class in progress. She did a double-take as she realized that the average age of the eleven women in the room had to be seventy.

"How wonderful," Mimi murmured as she watched the women bend and flow in graceful harmony and unity, their bodies lithe and supple in defiance of what those women had been conditioned for a lifetime to expect and accept.

"I started the sixty-plus group less than a year ago. Every one of these women has arthritis or heart disease or diabetes or some other debilitating malady, and most of them believed, when they first came here, that their physical life was over." Sylvia pointed to a gorgeous dark brown woman with close-cropped white hair in the center of the front row. "That's my mother. Sixty-eight. She's had two hip replacement operations and needed two canes to walk nine months ago. She's why I started the group. The three to her left are her bridge club." Sylvia laughed out loud and shook her head as she led Mimi past the studio to the front door.

"I knew yoga was one of those things that's supposed to be good for you, but I had no idea this was possible," Mimi said.

"It's better for you than lifting weights," Sylvia said in a totally non-proselytizing tone. "Come to a class sometime."

"Thanks," Mimi said. "I will." And she meant it.

The Boss was not happy and the entire Hate Crimes Unit knew it. She usually relaxed when she was with her Team in the privacy of the Think Tank, leaning back in her chair, feet on the desk, eyes closed, listening to them brainstorm, but she was conducting today's briefing like a college lecture. Bobby Gilliam always referred to this manifestation of Lieutenant Maglione as Her Chilly Self: when she grew still and quiet and her eyes flashed and her voice got so low she could barely be heard. Her Chilly Self had been that way since announcing to them that they were now Cowboy Cops. She obviously didn't share their elation at their change of fortune — which didn't unnerve them as much as their not being able to tell what Detective Ashby felt about it. He and the Lieutenant were so amazingly alike and yet so amazingly different that the Team was never more than fifty percent correct in their predictions of his reactions, responses and behaviors; but it was easier for them to know what to do when they could read Eric. The Boss and the Detective agreed and disagreed with each other at the most unlikely times. Cassie, Lynda and Bobby believed Eric to be secretly pleased to be a Cowboy. Tim and Kenny thought not.

They were grouped around the table in the Think Tank. Crime scene photos of the six murdered prostitutes lined one wall. The blackboard and the chart on the easel were filled with numbers and the codes that matched them with other numbers: telephone numbers, addresses, dates, times — all attempts to find points of commonality among the six dead women.

"Thanks to good work by everybody, we've made some real headway, Boss," Eric said en route to the blackboard. "It may or may not represent a pattern, but two women were killed in each of three locations: two worked the New York Avenue strip, two worked DuPont Circle East, and two worked downtown in the vicinity of the Convention Center and the train station." As he talked, he pointed to the photographs of the women and to the colored pins in the map that corresponded to the victim in question.

"What's the purple pin at the top of the map, Eric?" Gianna asked with a frown. That was a purely residential uptown area. "What's the connection?"

"That's a yoga and meditation center up in Takoma Park. Two of the victims had the phone number of this place among their possessions."

"Oh, practitioners of the New Age version of the world's oldest profession?"

A little laugh of relief swept the room. The Boss was thawing out, becoming her human self.

Eric grinned in relief too. "Kenny will be happy to tell you the whole story since he made the initial visit."

Gianna listened intently as Kenny detailed his visit to the Washington Center for Spiritual Awakening in an upper middle class section of the city adjacent to the Walter Reed Army Medical Center. She knew the area well: block after block of huge two- and-three-story Victorian homes, many of them restored to their former elegance by upwardly mobile and well-salaried young professionals. Ancient oaks and elms towered over the houses, giving the houses the appearance of being protected while also enhancing their graceful beauty. Takoma Park had been for a long time, if not always, a rather eclectic community in what was a largely staid and conservative city, so it wasn't surprising to find the Center for Spiritual Awakening located there. Nine people lived in the Center, Kenny related, all of whom taught several classes a week in yoga and meditation; all of whom volunteered at least two days a week working with the ill or the aged or the imprisoned; all of whom spent at least two evenings a week seeking to acquaint prostitutes with the dangers of AIDS.

"Are these people legit?" Gianna interrupted Kenny's report.

"As legit as you or me, Boss," Eric said. "I

checked 'em every way from Christmas and back. Not a single blemish on a single one of them. They're the real thing: truly decent people."

"Okay, Kenny," she said, signaling him to continue his report.

"When they go out on the street, when they pass out condoms, they also pass out free vegetarian meals to anybody who asks. And it seems they'll just sit and talk to anybody who needs to talk. Two of our victims — Sandra Ann King aka Shelley Kelley, and Patricia McIntire aka Patty Mack — got in real close with these Center people. Quit drinking and drugging and were about to quit the street life when they got offed."

"And do what?" Tim snorted. "Sell flowers at Union Station?"

"Hey, Man, I'm just telling you what the people told me," Kenny said with an elaborate shrug.

"Sounds a little too good to be true to me," Bobby offered. "I find it hard to believe that a plate of vegetables will make a junkie clean up, or a hooker stop tricking."

"Anybody can turn a life around at any time," Lynda said with a wise nod of her head. "My Uncle Hugo had a dream one night that an angel saved him from the fires of hell. The next week, he passed out drunk in an alley off Columbia Road, behind his favorite hangout. Some kids set him on fire. A lady heard him screaming and ran outside in her nightgown and poured water on him. She saved his life. She was his dream come true, you know, because she looked like an angel in her nightgown and all. Anyway, he hasn't had a drink since, and he's helped start three Spanish-speaking Alcoholics Anonymous meetings in Adams-Morgan."

"Bet he keeps his ass out of alleys, too," Bobby said, and even Lynda joined in the raucous laughter that lightened the mood in the room, extending even to Gianna.

"One other thing, Boss," Kenny said when order returned. "Even though the folks at that Spiritual Center uptown were really impressed that we're investigating these murders, I got the feeling that they were holding something back. So I thought..." He trailed off, looking slightly uncomfortable.

"You thought what, Kenny?" Gianna prodded.

"Well, I thought it might help if you went to talk to them, you being a Lieutenant and all..."

"Good idea." She rifled through the stack of reports, found his, and placed it on the top of the pile. "I'll go in the morning. Call and set it up for nine-thirty. Anything else jump out at us?"

"Yeah, Boss. One more thing." Eric opened a report from the Medical Examiner, took out a sheet of paper, and slid it across the table to Gianna. "Late March and early April, late September and early October. All the murders occurred in those months. I gotta think that's signifi —" He stopped speaking because she was no longer listening. Instead, her gaze was fixed on the blackboard, at the series of telephone numbers.

"That's certainly worth considering," she said. Her voice had gone tight again. She stood, gathered up the reports, and crossed to the door. "Eric, my office, please. Rest of you, good work."

"What the hell's eating her?" Bobby whispered

even though the door to the Think Tank was closed and Gianna and Eric were gone long enough to be halfway down the hall.

"I told you what. She's pissed off in a big way about us being moved into the Chief's office," Kenny said authoritatively.

"That's not why she was staring at these phone numbers like she was," Cassie said, positioning herself in front of the blackboard, scrutinizing the numbers. "Where was she looking? I swear she saw something that rang her bell . . ."

"Oh, Miss Thing, you are so dramatic." This from the drama queen extraordinaire. "I'll bet it's something domestic, like she's having problems with her lover," Tim added.

"You really think she's gay?" Bobby queried.

"Of course she is," Cassie and Tim insisted in unison.

"Well," Kenny offered, "we've never seen her with a guy."

"You've never seen me with a guy, either, and I'm not gay," Lynda shot at him with disdain. "That's a stupid thing to say, Kenny Chang."

"I've never seen you with anything but a crime report," Kenny shot back, stung by her reproach.

"But I have seen the lieutenant with a woman," Cassie casually threw into the conversational lull. "Saturday afternoon."

She had everyone's total and complete attention. "What's she look like?" asked Bobby.

"Major league fine," said Cassie with so much feeling that they all laughed at her. "There were four of them at this outdoor cafe. The lieutenant and her woman, and these other two women, and they were

92

all major league fine." Cassie described Mimi, Beverly and Sylvia in detail, and the way in which, at the end of the meal, Gianna joined Mimi in her red 1969 Karmann Ghia convertible. "What I wouldn't give for a woman like one of them," she said wistfully.

"Me too!" said Bobby with feeling.

"You gotta let the chips fall where they fall, Anna. You know that. Besides, what exactly are you worried about anyway?"

"I'm worried that if we ask why her phone number was in the possession of two murdered hookers, it'll rekindle her interest in the story. So far, Eric, she's at a dead end and has let the thing drop. I don't want her on this case, and I sure as hell don't want her to know we're working it." Gianna was still recovering from the shock of seeing Mimi's telephone number on the blackboard in the Think Tank beside the names Shelley Kelley and Starry Knight. "Besides. What the ever lovin' hell is she doing giving hookers her home telephone number?"

Eric laughed in spite of himself. The one thing he could not have imagined was his boss, the always-in-control Lieutenant Maglione, Her Chilly Self, having a fit of jealous pique. But if there was anybody who could raise her hackles and lower her defenses, it would be Montgomery Patterson.

He recalled his last meeting with her. It had been the reporter, not the police, who'd learned where a psychotic serial killer had taken the head of the Hate Crimes Unit hostage. In the process of finding where

Gianna was being held, Patterson had also discovered why Gianna was destined to be the killer's next victim. Revealing that reason would have meant "outing" Gianna, which Patterson flat-out refused to do when Eric pressed her, and she'd called him a little shit, right in front of the Chief. She'd also done a better job of going undercover than he had, and she'd generally been running neck and neck with the police as they investigated the murders. In addition to the fact that she was one gorgeous woman. It didn't surprise him that the Boss didn't want her lover chasing the killer of six prostitutes.

"It's Tim's call, Anna, and he'll handle it just like any other."

"Amazing, isn't it, how many serial killings are ritualistic."

It took him a moment to shift gears, to realize that she was onto another topic and she apologized when she saw the look on his face. "Sorry. My brain is roving. You said the murders all occurred in the spring and the fall —"

"No, I said March and October. You attached seasons."

"... spring and fall ... beginnings and endings ... alpha and omega." She was quiet for a moment. "It wouldn't surprise me if there was a seasonal connection to this thing," she continued. "Otherwise, why not whack 'em in January or June or December?"

"Why whack 'em at all?" he asked.

" 'Cause they're there and easy to whack," she answered.

"So are lots of other people."

"Yeah, but what do hookers represent, Eric?" And

she waited for him to join her thought process — something he often did — but when he didn't this time, she proffered her "fallen woman" theory, which, she suggested, could connect logically with a seasonal fixation if one assumed some cracked kind of religious motivation. He didn't buy it and said so.

"A woman-hating Jesus freak? Gimme a break, Anna." He yawned and apologized, then added, "I'm betting it's just another crazy, and I am, quite personally, getting sick and tired of 'em. I'd like to whack a few of them for a change. See how they like it."

She flipped open the top file on the stack and skimmed it. "Good for Kenny, by the way, suggesting that I follow-up on that Spiritual Center."

"You think it's good when the troops start giving orders to the boss?" He raised his eyebrows. "I can't wait to see how long this lasts."

"What's that supposed to mean? Haven't I always encouraged equal participation from the team?"

"Yeah, as long as everybody does everything your way, you're equal as they come," he said dryly.

"Speaking of which," she said, dismissing his comment, "Officer Ali is going to find herself on foot patrol if she isn't careful." And she filled him in on the tale of the Black Men On Guard carrying the truckload of Nazis away from Sophie Gwertzman's front door. And when he stopped laughing she told him she planned to put a female undercover on the street with the prostitutes to hear what the talk was about the murdered women, and correctly anticipated his response.

"Cassie and Lynda will have a joint fit and I won't hear the end of it until Christmas."

"It can't be helped, Eric. Neither of them has undercover experience and this isn't the case for on-the-job training. I need to get a woman on the street right away. September approaches..." She continued to go through the reports, reading with speed and assessing with clarity and asking pointed questions and accepting only those answers that made sense to her.

"You need to move faster on the Jane Does, Eric. We need to know like yesterday if six is the magic number or if there are more victims of this Daniel Boone Jesus-freak that we don't know about."

He stood up to leave. "I know, Boss. But things are a bit of a mess at the morgue —"

"Well, they're about to get messier, 'cause I also want you to order an analysis of the cause of death of every female who has come through the M.E. in the last three years." She deliberately did not look up from the report she was reading because she did not want to see the incredulity she knew was crowding his face.

When the door closed behind him, she checked the clock. She was scheduled to meet Mimi at the gym for a workout at eight. She had a meeting with Inspector Davis at six-thirty, which was in forty minutes. Time enough to read Kenny's report on the Spiritual Center and prepare for her visit there tomorrow — a prospect which was becoming more and more enticing. So was the thought of paying a visit to Yusuf Shakur and the B-MOGgers, and to the Training Academy to select a female undercover officer, and to Tyler Carson at the newspaper, and to the chief of forensics to talk about the pathology of serial killers of prostitutes — unfortunately a common

96

enough occurrence to have earned its own body of research and analysis. She was also looking forward to not wearing her uniform on a regular basis; to not feeling guilty about participating in her investigations instead of directing them; to not having to attend weekly crime stat analysis and update meetings. In short, she was allowing herself to feel the up side of being a cowboy cop, and she was, she had to admit to herself, enjoying the feeling.

It was already ninety degrees in most of Washington, but at least ten degrees cooler on the street where the Washington Center for Spiritual Awareness was located because the magnificent, ancient oaks and elms that lined the block on both sides of the street were so tall that their branches met in the middle of the street, providing a canopy of cool, green shade. Gianna arrived a little before nine-thirty, while some people were still leaving for work. Children and pets romped in the yards, as often as not running through the sprinklers that rotated in the hopes of saving expensive landscaping from the relentless heat. It struck Gianna as completely incongruous to arrive at such a bucolic setting for the sole purpose of discussing murder.

A small brass plaque on the front door of the house above the bell was the only indicator of the existence of the Center. Gianna pressed the bell and the door was opened almost immediately by a tiny, beautiful woman who appeared to be Native American. Raven black hair flecked with silver extended down her back to her hips. She wore a simple shift of yellow cotton and no shoes. She smiled at Gianna and beckoned her in.

"You would be the police lieutenant."

"Anna Maglione," Gianna said, offering her identification, which the woman waved away with a gentle, sweeping motion.

Gianna entered the foyer, noticed shoes neatly lined up, and removed her own. The woman, who had not yet identified herself, nodded her thanks, and led Gianna through a set of double doors into a massive and sparsely though warmly furnished room that Gianna imagined was probably used for meditation classes; it certainly wasn't the typical living room. A plush wall-to-wall off-white carpet covered the floor, and several exquisite kilim carpets lay on top. Half a dozen large pillows and three ottomans were placed strategically about the room. A long and comfortable-looking sofa was at one end of the room, in front of French doors that looked out onto a garden. A floor-to-ceiling bookshelf occupied the entire wall opposite the sofa. Only when she was in the room and seated on the sofa did Gianna realized that relaxing, meditative music was playing, but she saw no speakers in evidence.

"This is a wonderful room," Gianna said to the woman.

"Thank you, Lieutenant. It is used for group meditation classes and for lectures." The woman sat on an ottoman adjacent to the sofa. "I am Adrienne Lightfoot. I was advisor to Sandra and Patricia. I am both relieved and gratified to know that the police will not discard their deaths as society discarded their lives."

Gianna weighed her response carefully. It would be unwise to mislead this woman, just as it would be foolhardy to confirm her worst suspicions. "Miss Lightfoot, are you familiar with the work of the Hate Crimes Unit of the police department?"

"No, Lieutenant, I am not."

"I am the head of that unit. We investigate crimes against persons perpetrated because of race, religion, sexual orientation, and, with this case, gender. What I'm telling you, Miss Lightfoot, is that at least six prostitutes have been murdered and I think they were murdered simply and only because they were women."

Adrienne Lightfoot's eyes never left Gianna's, and they never wavered or changed expression. Then her lips lifted at the corners in a small smile. "I thought it was too good to be true that Sandra and Patricia of their own accord would generate such interest, but I am grateful for that interest no matter the reason. What can I do for you, Lieutenant?"

"You can tell me whatever you didn't tell Officer Chang. You can tell me everything you know about Sandra King and Patricia McIntyre. You can tell me whether those two women ever said anything that would give me a clue about who killed them and the other four. And you can tell me what the word is on the street among the prostitutes."

Gianna and Adrienne Lightfoot talked for an hour and a half, during which time the cowboy cop learned how much things had changed since her days on the street as a vice detective. AIDS and crack had made the streets not only meaner and scarier, but dangerous beyond comprehension. So dangerous that drug addicts were abandoning crack and returning to heroin, and prostitutes in increasing numbers were leaving the street life.

"They're such easy targets, those women," Adrienne said sadly. "By virtue of their presence they ask to be victimized, and there is absolutely no recourse. The shelters and jails and halfway houses and clinics cater overwhelmingly to men, and society still blames women for men's sickness."

And Adrienne Lightfoot finally told Gianna what she wanted to hear: That rumors had been floating about the street for over a year about a group of boys — college students, perhaps — who were required to kill a hooker as initiation into some kind of fraternal group or organization. No, Adrienne could not track down the source of the rumor. No, she did not remember when or from whom she first heard the rumor, only that it was at least a year ago. And no, she didn't know of any prostitute who would voluntarily talk to a police officer. It had taken seven months to gain the trust and confidence of Shelley and Patricia and now they were dead and word on the street was that not even yoga, meditation, and vegetables could save you when it was your time to go.

VII

When Mimi turned the corner onto her street, she saw the man standing on her front porch. She braked, shifted into neutral, and coasted down the street toward her house, her eyes on the man, tall and broad-shouldered, and definitely not anyone she knew. She saw him push the bell and await the response that would not come. She slowed virtually to a stop to watch, to see what he'd do next, to wonder who he was since he clearly wasn't delivering anything — no delivery truck in sight, and he wore a sport jacket and slacks. She eased to a stop directly in front of her house. The man removed a card from his pocket, wrote something on the back of it, and stuck it in the screen door. That's when Mimi got out of the car and strolled up the brick walkway to the steps. The man turned around. Good looking sucker.

"Hi. Can I help you?"

"Are you Marilyn Patterson?" he asked cheerfully.

"Who are you?" she asked, making no attempt to conceal her wariness. No one called her by her first name. No one outside her immediate family knew her first name.

He flipped open his police identification. "Officer Tim McCreedy, Metropolitan Police." He was still cheerful.

"I'm Montgomery Patterson, Officer. How can I help?"

"M. Montgomery Patterson? The reporter?" His good cheer evaporated.

"One and the same." She waited.

"Miss Patterson, your name was in the possession of two murder victims, Sandra Ann King and Stella Pearson . . ."

She cut him off. "I don't know anybody by those names."

Undeterred, he continued, ". . . also known as Shelley Kelley and Starry Knight." She noticed his pleasure at her reaction. "They were prostitutes," he said.

"Yes, Officer McCreedy, I know. Maybe you'd better come in."

She unlocked the door and ushered him into her study. She left him there while she opened the windows, turned on the fans front and back hoping for some kind of cross breeze, and brought bottles of mineral water for them.

She sat at the desk chair and motioned him into the overstuffed armchair adjacent to the bookshelf. "I guess I knew something had happened to them when I couldn't find them. But I guess I was also hoping that whatever it was, it wouldn't be this."

"When did you last see them, either of them, Miss Patterson?"

"Not for months. I lost touch with them sometime in March, maybe. I remember that it was still cold." At her last meeting with Shelley, a foot of snow had covered the ground and the temperature was in the single digits, and the girl wore spike heels and a spandex body suit and some kind of pretend fur coat, no hat and no gloves. And Starry had called her at home that same week, to cancel their meeting. She had the flu and wasn't on the street . . . and that was the last she'd seen or heard from either of them.

"Were they in any kind of trouble? Did they mention anything that would lead you to believe they were in any danger?"

Mimi hesitated, deciding what, if anything, she'd tell him. Not that she knew much. But she also wanted to know what he knew and she'd have to give up something to get something. "They'd been stringing me along for a while with the promise of a big story. I never got the details, just the hint that important men were somehow involved. How were they killed?"

"Knifed," said McCreedy, a little too quickly, Mimi thought.

"When were they killed?" she asked.

"Shelley in early April, Starry some time in late

March. Look, Miss Patterson, if you think of anything else, will you call me —" He stopped short, surprised, when she laughed.

"Not bloody likely, Officer. I do have my priorities, you know." He grinned back at her, causing her to think once again what he good-looking guy he was. He finished off his seltzer, gave her the bottle, and stood up to leave. He came face-to-face with the bookshelf, eye-to-eye with the photograph of Gianna there, and when he turned to her it was with a puzzled expression on his face. The grin was gone.

"Ah, Miss Patterson, did I ah, mention to you that I'm with the Hate Crimes Unit?"

She looked from him to the photo of Gianna and back to him. "Shit."

"Me, too," he said with feeling, and found his own way out, closing the door gently behind him.

"Shit!" Mimi said again, and at least four more times, each time louder than the preceding time.

She cursed the heat as she stripped out of the wilted clothes she'd worked in all day and made for the shower. She cursed Gianna's stubbornness for insisting that the two of them keep their professional lives separate from their personal lives. She cursed the fact that Officer McCreedy had to turn his pretty blue eyes right on Gianna's picture. Now one of Gianna's subordinates would know that his boss's photo was on some woman's bookshelf. But she stopped cursing when she realized, happily, that thanks to Officer McCreedy she now knew Shelley and Starry's real names and since they probably were D.C. natives she could ask Bev to run them through the school system's computer . . . Shit! Bev no longer worked for the school system. And come to think of

104

it, when she fixed the image of Officer McCreedy in her mind, if he wasn't gay she wasn't, and since she certainly was, so was he ... And so the hell what!

She dried herself and wondered why she had bothered to shower. When it was this hot in D.C., being perpetually drenched in sweat was a fact of life. She threw on a pair of cotton drawstring pants, a T-shirt, and sandals. She was scheduled to meet Sylvia for dinner and a briefing on what she'd learned about whoever was converting prostitutes. On her way out, she saw McCreedy's card still stuck in the screen door. She snatched it out and saw the familiar shield of the Metropolitan Police Department, read his name, and the words Hate Crimes Unit. Words that always said to her eyes and to her mind and to her heart, *Lieutenant Anna Maglione.* Gianna. She would, she decided in that moment, go to Gianna when she left Sylvia, and tell her about McCreedy, tell her that she planned to pursue the prostitute story, tell her that they needed to solve the dilemma of their lives. Beverly's words replayed themselves in her memory: *What you two do is too intense not to share it with each other.* She was right. It was not possible for them to compartmentalize their lives, not without compromising the health and growth of their relationship.

Mimi liked Sylvia more each time she saw her or talked with her and she was grateful that Beverly had found someone so wonderful. They had dinner at the Tandoor Oven on Connecticut Avenue, having discovered they both had a passion for Indian food.

The full-blast air conditioning more than compensated for the heat generated by the flame-throwing oven in the center of the room which gave the establishment its name. But the gist of the conversation Mimi found to be a downer, for Sylvia adamantly discouraged her from even attempting to approach the Washington Center for Spiritual Awareness.

"In the first place, Gianna beat you to it, and they're more than satisfied to leave the entire matter in the hands of the police. In the second place, the prostitutes are scared silly. They'll barely even talk to the Center staff any more." And with that, Sylvia refused further discussion of the matter, except to add that she'd offered her services to the Center, and to answer before Mimi asked: No, she would not ask any questions of the women on the street on Mimi's behalf. And that, Mimi sighed, was that.

Gianna opened the door peering over the reading glasses that rode low on her nose, and the quizzical expression that occupied her lovely face turned instantly to a grin of delight.

"What are you doing here?" she exclaimed, pulling Mimi inside and into a wonderful embrace, made more wonderful by the fact that Gianna was wearing jogging shorts and a tank top and nothing else.

"I apologize for arriving unannounced and uninvited and for disturbing your work," Mimi whispered from within the embrace, wishing that she didn't have to say what she'd come to say, wishing that she could just remain close in Gianna's arms.

"I'm paying bills," Gianna growled, waving one

arm toward the pile of papers on the dining room table, "so, your presence is a wonderful diversion. Have you eaten? You look wonderful, by the way."

"Just finished. Had dinner with Sylvia. And so do you."

"You like her, don't you," Gianna said, as she poured them tall, frosty glasses of lemonade and brought them to the sofa where Mimi was already sprawled, grateful for the air-conditioned coolness of Gianna's apartment, a welcome contrast to her heat- and humidity-ridden house. She'd have to invest in central air . . .

"She's wonderful, and I'm really happy for Bev. Gianna . . . can I tell you right now why I'm here?"

Gianna looked at her, the worry crease taking its place in the center of her forehead, and Mimi laughed, reached out to smooth it away. "Don't look like that. It's not *that* serious. But we do need to talk. Okay?"

"Okay," Gianna said, the crease returning with the concern at the tone of Mimi's words.

"Officer McCreedy paid me a visit this evening."

"Ah," Gianna said.

"You knew he was coming?"

"Yes," Gianna said.

"Would it have been so terrible if you'd told me?"

"How could I have done that without involving my private life in my professional life?" Gianna asked, and it was a genuine question.

"Gianna, we've got to find a way to share our work without violating our professional ethics. I don't want to hide my work from you. I want you to know what I'm doing, I want to share that with you, and I believe I can do that in such a way that I don't compromise either of us. I wish you shared that belief." Mimi watched and waited as Gianna processed her words and processed her own thoughts and formulated a response.

"You know what my first thought was when I saw your number written on the blackboard, Mimi? I wanted to know what the hell some other woman was doing with it."

"Sounds like a jealous hissy fit, which I'd have loved to receive, by the way, but it honestly doesn't seem like private life threatening the work ethic."

Gianna let a small grin turn her lips upward as she continued. "Then I was pissed off that you were involved in this case, and then I got scared that once again we'd find ourselves on a collision course . . ."

She didn't need to complete the thought because she knew they both remembered vividly their parallel investigation into the murders of four wealthy and deep-in-the-closet gay people a year ago that almost destroyed their relationship before they'd really gotten it going. And since then, they'd avoided, at Gianna's insistence, discussing their work beyond surface issues; and for a year, that tactic had worked. Until now. Until, once again, they were investigating the same case.

"I had dinner with Sylvia because I like her, yes, but also because I'd asked her to help me gather some information."

A wide range of emotions swept across the soft contours of Gianna's face and plumbed the depths of her hazel eyes, the final one being recognition. Perhaps five seconds had elapsed. "The Washington

Center for Spiritual Awareness," she said, and it was a statement and not a question.

"Damn, Lieutenant, you're good," Mimi said with admiration and respect in the laugh that she couldn't stop from coming.

"And?" Gianna raised her eyebrows awaiting a response.

"And you'd already beat me to the punch and the Center people not only won't talk to me, they won't talk to anybody. So, it's back to square one for me." Mimi sighed.

"What about your friend, Baby?"

Mimi almost giggled. "Baby wants to get paid."

"So? Pay her," Gianna said nonchalantly.

"Reporters don't pay for information, Gianna," Mimi said almost rudely, and was instantly glad that she'd restrained herself when she saw the look on Gianna's face.

"They don't? What about all those investigative programs on television and the tabloids —"

"That shit's not journalism," Mimi snarled, "it's all hype and sensationalism and it's got nothing to do with what I do!"

Gianna quickly and solemnly apologized. She realized that she'd made a major error and wished to correct it immediately. It took several moments before Mimi's calm was restored and they could continue their conversation, one they both were working hard to keep free of anger or recrimination.

"McCreedy saw your photograph on my book-shelf."

"Oh, shit."

"That's what I said. That's what he said."

"Oh, shit," Gianna said again and got up to pace a few steps before coming back to stand before Mimi. "I suppose if I'd let you know that we'd found your phone number . . ."

"That I'd have stuffed your photo into a drawer before McCreedy's fine self appeared at my door?" Mimi grinned and shrugged. "I don't know, darling, but I do know the guy wouldn't have caught me by surprise. And yes, if I thought it really mattered to you, I'd have moved the photo."

Gianna regarded her intently, then sat down close beside her and took her hand. "You're right, of course."

"I am?" Mimi widened her eyes in an exaggerated display of surprise. "Hallelujah! Write this down: date, time, place. The lieutenant said I was right about something!" She laughed as Gianna grabbed her, pushed her back into the sofa, and bit her neck. "So if I'm right, does that mean you admit to being wrong?"

"Don't push your luck, Patterson." Gianna attempted to growl and sound threatening, but it came out more of a giggle instead, and they both knew they'd opened a big door. Opened it so wide that Gianna comfortably settled back into Mimi's arms and told her all about being a cowboy cop . . .

VIII

When Gianna opened the door to the Think Tank
for the eight o'clock weekly Unit meeting on the
second Monday in September all talk ceased and
mouths from which words had been flowing freely the
moment before hung open at the sight of her.
"What's wrong with you people? Never seen a cowboy
before?"

Gianna wore loose fitting black jeans, black
snakeskin cowboy boots — a wonderfully extravagant
gift from Mimi to celebrate what she thought was a
big step up for Gianna — a white shirt, and her usual

111

under-the-arm holster. She crossed to her customary place at the head of the long table, sat down, put her cowboy-booted feet up on the table and accepted the mug of coffee Tim gave her; he always had it ready and waiting. She sipped from the cup and waited for Eric to get started, impatient because she had a meeting in an hour with the two undercover cops working the Daniel Boone killings, and she'd promised to make a personal visit to the Office of Latino Affairs to hear firsthand complaints that investigators from the Immigration and Naturalization Service were once again staging illegal raids on restaurants and hotels downtown looking for undocumented workers. She'd also promised to look into why the city's Department of Public Works, after three weeks, still hadn't removed the swastikas and other graffiti spray-painted on the wall of the down-town Hebrew Academy.

"Nice boots, Boss," Cassie offered.

"Thanks," Gianna said shortly, reaching for the ever-expanding stack of files. "And may I assume that there's something here from the ME's office?" she asked, even as she found what she was looking for, and it took about three seconds for the gist of the analysis to reach her understanding. "Fuck a duck," she exclaimed under her breath, and looked up over her reading glasses to chastise whoever had snickered. But her heart wasn't in it.

The raw truth staring her in the face had knocked the wind out of her: the three-year analysis of cause of death in females from 1 January 1991 to the present indicated that a total of nine women had died from knife wounds to the chest. Gianna studied the pattern of the murders: one in April of 1991; two in October of 1991; one each in March and October of 1992; then one each in March and September of 1993; and one each in March and April of 1994. In three of the cases, the knives had been removed from the bodies prior to discovery. Four of the cases remained Jane Does.

Gianna removed her reading glasses and slid them into her shirt pocket. Having to wear them all the time when reading was a new reality in her life and it annoyed her more than she had words to express. Now she'd need to add the Chief to her list of meetings for the day, to let him know that the serial killer had struck nine times, not six, as they'd first believed.

"Cassie," she said, standing up, "meet me at the Public Works Department at two-thirty, director's office. Lynda, you meet me at Latino Affairs at three-thirty, general counsel's office. The rest of you and Eric, try to find out how much of a waste of time it will be to reconstruct the case files on these victims."

She left them, not caring that she'd not concealed from her voice a single trace of the disgust she felt.

The notorious Central Cell Block, in the basement of Police Headquarters, was every bit as disgusting as the general public had always imagined it to be. It was old, it was dirty, and it stank. One of the perks Gianna enjoyed as a lieutenant was never again having to process a perp in Central. So, she was accompanied by a wave of unfond memories as she took the elevator to the basement and it was a good thing that the intake officer with whom she checked her weapon knew her and knew why she was there because she'd never have recognized the two undercovers she found waiting for her in the interview cell.

They'd responded to her summons coming directly off shift, and thought it better to meet her in Central where they looked like they belonged. When she'd met them at the training academy a month ago — six-year veteran Tony Watkins and four-year veteran Alice Long — they looked exactly like the smart, dedicated young Vice cops they were. At this moment, they looked like they should be in Central lockup waiting for a court appearance. Tony's toes were poking out of the holes in filthy sneakers with no laces — toes without socks. His trousers were encased with ancient specimens of grease and grime and were held up with a length of equally slimy rope. He appeared to wear at least three shirts, each more ragged than the other, and a jacket that seemed almost clean by comparison. The color of everything he wore was neither discernible nor recognizable. He looked exactly like a man who lived on the street. Only the closest inspection would reveal, in the middle of the scraggly, raggedy beard, beautiful white teeth and, above the beard, clear, sparkling, intelligent brown eyes, and Tony Watkins would never permit anyone on the street to get that close to him. His three shirts and jacket concealed the bulk of the 9mm Glock revolver in the holster under his arm.

Alice, on the other hand, was at least clean, if equally bizarre in her attire. She wore the body-hugging spandex favored by prostitutes — black with black fishnet stockings and six-inch orange patent leather heels to match the two-foot-long hair that cascaded down her back. She had on so much make-up that her features were totally distorted. Gianna knew she was Alice only because of her distinctive South Carolina coastal accent, and because of the spectacular body hugged by the spandex. Alice was a knockout.

Both officers stood when Gianna entered the room, and she waved them back down. They'd been awake all night and needed the rest. She noticed that they both had cups of coffee and the remains of food of some kind. They looked tired, and she was glad, when she looked at them, that she'd decided to put Tony in as back-up for Alice. They'd only been out for three weeks, but clearly the job was taking its toll.

"What's up, Lieutenant?" Tony threw her a friendly salute.

"My blood pressure," Gianna said with feeling, and they both grinned. "But you're here to help that, I hope."

"I think we got somethin' for you," Alice said in the soft rhythm of the Gullah people of the islands off the South Carolina coast. She detailed for Gianna the activities of a black Jeep Wrangler that had cruised the downtown streets near the bus station and the convention center and the train station for the last two weekends. Just on Friday and Saturday nights. At least two young white men in the vehicle at all times, sometimes three, sometimes four. Sometimes the top was off and the boys were visible, sometimes not. "I hollered at 'em one time," Alice said, "tryin' to get 'em to pull over. But one of the other girls said those boys been drivin' by like that

115

for quite some time and they don't ever stop. None of the girls had ever seen or heard of them even slowin' down to talk, to say nothin' of buyin' trade."

"They've been cruising for quite some time, you said. How long, Alice?" Alice and Tony had no way of knowing that Gianna's laid-back, almost lazy manner of questioning was a sure signal that every fiber of her was on full alert.

"One of the girls said at least a year," Alice responded.

Gianna considered the report she'd read not an hour earlier and wished she'd had more time to spend with it before having to meet Tony and Alice. Would there be a hit in September or would it come in October? And at which of the locations noted for street-walking prostitutes would be the most likely target? She was reluctant to move Alice and Tony at this juncture, but if she had to . . .

"You called them boys, Alice. How old?"

She didn't hesitate. "I'd bet not a one of 'em's over twenty," she said, and looked to Tony for confirmation.

He nodded, and picked up the story. "I got up off the bench one night when they passed by and the top was down and the traffic light caught 'em at the intersection of Ninth and G. Walked right up to the truck, stumbled into it, looked right into their faces. Alice is right. Nothin' but boys. And rich boys, I'd say, by the look of 'em."

Gianna questioned them thoroughly, took them through the paces several times, checking and double-checking their information, and she agreed that the Jeep and its occupants constituted a strong lead. She wrote down the number of the Virginia license plate of the truck and the descriptions of the boys, though she knew Alice and Tony both would submit fully detailed reports. She'd also have them get with the artist later in the day to work up some sketches.

"What's the mood on the street, Alice? Are the women nervous at all?"

"Hard to say, Lieutenant. You know, actin' tough out on those streets is a major part of survival, so you can't ever tell for sure when somebody's really brave or just actin' brave or so full of crack they don't know the difference. But I'll tell you this: the sooner you pull us in, the better. They might not be scared, but I am, and when I come in, it'll be a long while before I volunteer for undercover unless it's in a bank or somewhere safe."

"Me, too," Tony said, anger puncturing his easy-going voice. "Some little fucker tried to torch me the other night. I felt him trying to check my pockets, which was all right. I wouldn't have let him get close enough to touch my piece. Then I smelled something and before I could register it was gasoline, he'd lit the match. Good thing Long Legs here was walking toward me. She saw what was happening and chased him down. Caught him, too, and smacked him upside the head." Tony almost grinned at the memory, but it was too painful for real humor. "He was a kid, Lieutenant. I mean like seven or eight." He shook his head. "How can somebody be that depraved that young?" Then a grin did break over his face and the perfect white teeth and beautiful brown eyes sparkled and Gianna remembered that he was quite a handsome man. "You shoulda seen the look on that little bastard's face when Alice ran him down. She's a marathoner, you know. That's why I call her Long

117

Legs. Boston *and* New York. Ran him down in a flaming red pair of those come-fuck-me's and grabbed him and smacked him so hard I'll bet his teeth are still rattling."

Gianna laughed all the way back to her office, the image of Officer Alice Long — Long Legs — in six-inch flaming red spike heels running after and catching an eight-year-old boy as clear in her mind as the shock on the child's face when the hooker outran him, caught him, and then smacked him. She stopped laughing when another image crowded in: that of Officer Tony Watkins soaked in gasoline and a breath away from a lighted match.

It had taken Mimi a full week to locate Beverly's friend in the school system's administrative office, and then to get her on the phone long enough to arrange a meeting. That she fully understood the hectic beginning of the school year did nothing to lessen her growing impatience with the need to break some new ground in her investigation of the disappearance and death of Starry Knight and Shelley Kelley and the other women who were Baby's friends. She would have to break new ground or yield to the ever-increasing pressure of her editors to accept other assignments.

Tyler was still pushing for her to look into the proliferation of the white supremacist groups, and she was still adamantly refusing, citing not only the potential for danger to herself as a Black woman, but her absolute lack of interest in the subject. The editor who was technically her boss, when Mimi wasn't circumventing him to work with Tyler, was pushing an illegal aliens story. Mimi had responded that she'd be happy to investigate why the government seemed to have one set of laws governing the entry of immigrants from Europe and Asia, and another philosophy altogether when the arrival of people from the Caribbean and South and Central America was the issue . . . people who were called aliens, and not immigrants. She had pissed off her editor in a big way with her attitude: "Those Haitians and Salvadoreans are busting their asses cleaning hotel rooms and washing dishes for minimum wage and you want me to watch the INS bust their asses for lack of a green card? Want me to tell you who the real criminals are?"

She was skating on thin ice and she knew it. There were only so many stories swimming around in the pond at any one time, and she'd have to haul one of them out in a big hurry if she was to keep her hotshot status. She was convinced that the story of the dead hookers was a big, big fish swimming in deep water; but until McCreedy's visit, she'd been fishing without bait. Now she had their names — their real names — and the belief that at least a couple of them had to have been D.C. natives. Yes, young women flocked to Washington from small towns and cities in Virginia and Maryland, and from other southern states and, for any number of reasons, ended up prostituting themselves. But the odds were better than good that a couple of them began and ended their lives right here, and public school records would tell her that.

Convincing Beverly's friend to do a records search proved to be almost as daunting as a conversation with Baby. First, Mimi had to convince the woman that she did not want the academic or any other personal records of any of the women. Then, when she had explained in detail the nature of the story, she had to convince the woman that no story she wrote would cast the D.C. public schools in a negative light: of course the school system couldn't be faulted for the lives its former students chose for themselves. All Mimi wanted, she explained with all the patience remaining to her, was an address, the name of a parent, a social security number, anything that would help her track down Sandra King and Stella Pearson. Yes, she understood that people moved, but perhaps a neighbor would remember and have a forwarding address. And no, Mimi would not reveal the name of her source, would not even indicate a contact with the school system. Finally, Mimi persuaded the woman to call her with the information in three days. Then, to rid herself of the pent-up frustration from dealing with the school's administrator, she walked the mile and a half to Police Headquarters. A couple of Vice guys she'd worked stories with for years might help, and unless they were in court, she expected that they'd be hunched over their desks completing paperwork that never seemed to end.

She called from the pay phone on the ground floor of the building. Some cops didn't want to be seen talking to her, a fact of life which pissed her off no end but which she'd learned to accept. The problem stemmed from a series of articles she'd written two years ago exposing a cell of rogue cops who'd designated themselves judge, jury and executioner in a misguided effort to rid the streets of drug dealers. Mimi, thus, was viewed as the enemy by those cops who believed that any word against anybody in blue was the equivalent of a declaration of war.

"Ernie, this is Montgomery Patterson."

"Yo, Patterson. Who're you puttin' the sting to today?"

"Not stinging today, Ernie, just searching. I'm downstairs. I need to talk to you. You coming to me or do you want me to come there up?"

"Hell no! I don't need to be caught talking to you. Meet me downstairs in the cafeteria."

Mimi walked down the stairs to the basement, resenting like hell his treatment of her, even though she suspected his ill humor was due in equal parts to overwork and to his not wanting to be identified as a reporter's source.

Nobody she knew ate the food in the Police Department cafeteria. Because, Mimi was convinced, it wasn't really food. No matter when she had been here — and granted it wasn't a regular occurrence — whatever was being served looked exactly like what was being served the time before. She observed that the people eating looked like visitors to the building — they looked like lawyers or relatives or perps — they did not look like cops or parole officers or people who worked in the building. She studied a bottle of apple juice that claimed to be one hundred percent pure and free from preservatives, decided to trust it, and was paying the cashier when Ernie walked in. He joined her at the front of the line, also bypassing the food at the steam table, paid for a cup of coffee and a doughnut, and followed her to a table in the far corner of the room.

Ernie looked worse than when she last saw him. He smoked, drank and ate too much, and was now at least fifty pounds overweight. She couldn't imagine him running down a perp. His neck and chins crowded his shirt collar and the loosened tie. His face showed scratches and the missed places from his shave that morning. Stringy blond hair refused to stay out of his eyes, no matter how often he pushed it away.

"You look like shit, Ernie."

"Fuck you, Patterson. I got too much work to do to take shit from you. Whaddya want?"

"How's Ralph?" Mimi refused to be intimidated by Ernie. She'd tell him what she wanted when she felt like it.

"Tryin' to decide whether or not he's glad he ain't dead. Caught a bullet about a month back. Messed his insides all to hell. Poor bastard never will have a normal shit again."

Ralph and Ernie had been partners for over a decade and Mimi now understood at least part of the reason for Ernie's appearance. Not only was Ernie carrying the grief of having a partner downed, he was probably carrying a big load of guilt as well. Mimi would bet that Ernie had been close enough to Ralph to have caught a bullet as well, and knew that it could have been his insides instead of Ralph's that had been rearranged.

"I'm really sorry, Ernie. Give him my regards."

"Thanks, Patterson. I will. Now. Whaddya want?"

Mimi began to tell him what she knew about the murdered prostitutes but he stopped her before she got very far. "We ain't got 'em no more. That pushy broad in Hate Crimes has 'em. Some cockamamie bullshit about it bein' a hate crime to off some junkie hookers." Ernie drained his cup and pushed back his chair.

Mimi's brain was reeling from hearing Gianna described as a pushy broad, while at the same time trying to figure a way to keep Ernie from rushing off. "But you had 'em at one time, right?" she queried hastily.

"A couple of 'em."

"Sandra King and Stella Pearson?"

"Sandra King and Andrea Thomas. I remember the Thomas broad 'cause she was a Jane Doe for a lotta weeks. And that's all I remember, Patterson. I gotta go."

Ernie finished his doughnut, wiped his mouth with his hand, and heaved his bulk out of the chair and lumbered across the room. He stopped halfway to the door, turned, and came back to loom over her, a scowl etching the hangover in his face.

"I don't know why I'm bothering to help you out on this one, Patterson. But just so you get it right, they weren't knifed. Not in the way you mean it."

"How many ways are there, Ernie?"

"Well, if you're a modern day Daniel Boone, you throw a six-inch hunting knife into the heart from a moving car." Then Ernie turned and retraced his steps, this time getting all the way to and out of the door.

A six-inch hunting knife. And, if she was adding correctly, five victims now, instead of four.

Mimi left Police Headquarters with a headache. There was too much to balance and her brain wasn't up to trying. She had to stifle an urge to pop in on Gianna. She didn't like hearing her referred to negatively, and she wondered if that was the prevailing attitude among the cops, that she was a pushy broad. The sinking feeling at that prospect was joined by a momentary something that resembled sympathy for Gianna: Some asshole was killing women by throwing hunting knives into them from moving vehicles and Gianna had to find him in the face of hostile resentment from her own colleagues.

And, of course, she was furious at once again having had Gianna shut all the doors to the case, meaning weeks of grunt work for Mimi with no promise at all of any payoff. No wonder she had a headache. It wasn't normal to be in love with a woman, and feel sorry for her, all the while being furious at her. She jaywalked across the street to the Department of Motor Vehicles. A sometime source there might be willing to check and see if any of the women had a driver's license.

It took forty minutes to locate the guy, a supervisor in the Traffic Adjudication section, and another hour of sitting through hearings waiting for the lunch break, an hour during which she heard every excuse imaginable for why people failed to pay their traffic tickets. And after all the waiting, what she got was a possible maybe that he'd have time to run the names through the computer for her. That and a dark warning about violating the private rights of citizens. She checked her irritation at the civics lesson and gave him the list of three names she'd jotted down.

"Andrea Thomas? What do you want with her?" The suspicion in his voice gave her a quick rush of adrenaline.

"You know her?" Mimi kept the interest in her voice casual.

"I know her sister. She works in records. What do you want with Andrea Thomas?"

Mimi could sense that she was losing him, and she'd have to tell him something to keep him from backing off. "She was murdered. I'm just trying to collect some background information, something that might point to a reason."

"She was a junkie and a hooker. Two good reasons right there. Some pimp or some john offed her. Who cares?"

"I do," Mimi said through clenched teeth, "if it's the same pimp or john who offed her and a few others."

He shrugged, and said, "All the same to me," and turned to walk away. Over his shoulder he called out, "You owe me one, Patterson."

"Not bloody likely," Mimi muttered to herself, and, cursing bureaucrats with a new found vehemence, was about to head off when a thought struck her and she rushed down the hall to catch up with him, pushing through the crowd that always seemed to overwhelm the Motor Vehicles Department.

"What's her name," Mimi panted when she caught up with him.

"Whose name?" He looked at her as if at a crazed stranger.

"The sister. The one who works in records."

"Gwen," he said. "And you didn't get that from me."

* * * * *

Mimi spent another two days looking for Gwen Thomas and when she found her, she almost regretted the effort. Over the years, during the course of her investigations, Mimi had encountered dozens of people who were afraid to talk to reporters, who didn't like reporters, who resented reporters intruding into their lives. And on rare occasions she'd encountered someone like Gwen Thomas who quite simply had no respect for journalists and their work, and that was always hard to take. Mimi could honestly say that while she knew a hell of a lot of *people* for whom she had no respect — individuals she could call by name — with the exception of drug dealing, she couldn't think of a single *profession* for which she had no respect.

She'd asked around and had Gwen Thomas pointed out to her and had introduced herself and followed the woman outside on her lunch break.

Gwen Thomas had brushed off Mimi's approach with casual politeness and without a trace of anger or hostility. "I have nothing to say to you, Miss Patterson."

Mimi studied the woman. She was attractive and intelligent and the pain that crossed her face when Mimi mentioned Andrea's name made it clear that she had loved her murdered sister.

"It is possible, Miss Thomas, that your sister's death was not an isolated incident."

Mimi watched the other woman's expression closely to see how this information registered, but it was she who got the surprise when Gwen Thomas said, "I know that. So does Lieutenant Maglione. She's the one you should be talking to anyway, not me." And Gwen Thomas melted into the lunch-hour pedestrian traffic in front of the Municipal Center.

Mimi stood there, in the way of the hordes of people shuttling to and from lunch, thinking about how much more open she and Gianna had been with each other in recent weeks about their work. Gianna had told her all about the move into the Chief's office, about the Black Men On Guard and the neo-Nazis, about giving the Gwertzman story to Tyler in the first place, about the undercover cop in six-inch red spike heels chasing and catching the eight-year-old torcher. But Gianna would never, ever, share with her the real details of her work. Like the fact that hunting knives had been thrown at the victims from passing cars ... And Mimi could only admit the truth: that she had no right to expect it.

She sighed heavily and then, suddenly, brightened. The fact that Gianna was always several steps ahead of her on this story had given her the gut feeling that the hooker murder story was a big fish swimming in the deep water. What Ernie had just told her about the hunting knives confirmed it. Now all she needed to do was come up with enough solid facts to sell the story to the editors.

IX

Gianna called the Second District watch commander and left an urgent message for Alice and Tony: she needed to hear from them the moment they checked in, and she didn't care what time it was. She left her home number and hung up, returning her focus to the report before her.

The license check showed that the black Jeep Wrangler was registered to a member of the United States House of Representatives from Utah. If there was a mistake, Gianna wanted to know now.

The license check also revealed outstanding

parking tickets dating back three years totaling more than fifteen hundred dollars, most of which had become warrants for arrest. And that was just in D.C. She'd run a check in the morning, to determine whether Virginia or Maryland had anything. But first she wanted to double-check with Alice and Tony, though deep within her she knew there was no mistake. They weren't the kind of cops to make mistakes. If they said that was the license number, then it was.

And that meant that a member of Congress somehow was involved in the murders of nine prostitutes.

She was in the Think Tank, where she spent most of her time these days. Because her reassignment relieved her of the pressure of giving speeches and compiling crime statistics and analytical reports, she was no longer confined to her office doing the work of an administrator. She stood, stretched, and walked over to the map that showed the locations where the nine victims had been found. Something puzzled her and she stood there several long minutes trying to figure out what. The phone rang and she looked over at it and saw that it was her private line. She looked up at the clock, relieved to see that she wasn't late for her meeting with the Chief.

"Lieutenant Maglione," she answered.

"I gotta go to a meeting with the mayor tonight, Maglione," the Chief barked into the phone without preamble. "See me tomorrow at lunch time. I'll order you one of those veggie burger things you like."

And she was left holding a dial tone, her mouth still forming the words to tell him that she needed to see him tonight, to tell him how much bigger the problem was, that it could reach all the way to the Congress of the United States. But he was gone.

She returned to the map and traced with her finger the line that was New York Avenue, then the lines that were the streets that fed into Thomas Circle, then the lines that were the streets that fed into DuPont Circle — the areas of heaviest street prostitution and the areas where all the victims . . . and there was the answer.

She looked at the nine red pins that signified the nine victims. Each pin was located two or three blocks away from the action strip, away from the main drag. The prostitutes were killed *near* the main drags, not on them. Did that mean that nine women had been lured away from the main drag and onto side streets? Or had they been just unlucky enough to get caught in an isolated situation?

Gianna crossed to her desk and picked up the phone. As she waited for the number to connect she pulled the file on the black Jeep Wrangler toward her. She identified herself to the WASIS technician who answered, and gave him the access code that authorized her to solicit information from the Washington Area Shared Information System — a sophisticated computerized data bank of information on crime and criminals that combined the law enforcement efforts of D.C. and the Maryland and Virginia suburbs. The system contained every scrap of information contained in every report submitted during the investigation of every crime: every statement, every phone number and license number, every address, every date of birth of every person interviewed, and whether a suspect ever had been interviewed in connection with another crime in that jurisdiction. Because the WASIS information was so detailed and so invasive, a certain level of authority was required to access it. There were ten levels of authority that qualified. Gianna had eight levels of clearance.

She gave the technician the license number of the Jeep and he advised her if WASIS had anything, she could expect it tomorrow afternoon.

Feeling a lightness she didn't understand until she realized it was relief at not having to meet with the Chief, she turned out the lights in the Think Tank and went to meet Mimi, Freddie and Cedric for dinner at Freddie's restaurant — where the chef always concocted special vegetarian dishes for her and Mimi — and for billiards at a classy new joint owned by a former Redskin teammate of Freddie's.

When the beeper went off, Mimi, Gianna and Freddie all put down their cue sticks and reached for their belts and their little black beepers.

Cedric looked at them and shook his head. "You are pathetic, the lot of you." He started to say more until he noted the look on Gianna's face.

The beeper was hers and her face grew more and more serious as she read the message being transmitted on the tiny screen. She reset the beeper and returned the gadget to its place on her belt.

"Officer down," she said quietly. Then, turning to Mimi, she added, "Somewhere in the Fifth District."

Mimi knew that Gianna was feeling what all cops feel when they learn that one of their own has been injured, and she understood that it was important to know who and how serious it was. She just wished sometimes that it didn't intrude so much. All high-ranking officials were informed of the occurrence of certain events, a downed officer being one of them. That knowledge would cast a pall over Gianna for the rest of the evening and a part of Mimi resented it.

The three of them simultaneously reached for their belts when, several minutes later, a beeper sounded again; and again it was Gianna's. This time as she read the message being printed on the mini screen all the color drained from her face and her hand shook slightly.

"I have to go. Mimi I'll call you later..." She was across the room and out of the door before Mimi caught up to her.

"Gianna, for God's sake, what is it?"

"Cassandra Ali is the officer down."

She rushed out of the pool room, followed by Mimi, Cedric, and Freddie, who was offering to drive her to the hospital since she didn't have her car. In one of those rare and truly blessed moments, a patrol car came cruising down the block. Gianna sprinted for it, flashed her badge at the officer riding shotgun and told him who she was and what she wanted. The car's driver had activated lights and siren before Gianna was even in the car, and the noise obliterated Gianna's shout to Mimi that she would call her later.

The Chief and Inspector Davis were the first people Gianna saw when she burst through the double doors of the crowded emergency room of the Washington Hospital Center.

"What happened?" she asked, the breath caught painfully in her chest.

"Somebody beat her up pretty bad, Anna, but we don't know who or why," Inspector Davis answered for the two senior officials.

"How bad?" Gianna demanded.

"She's alive and she'll live," the Chief answered. "But it's bad, Lieutenant. It's real bad."

She couldn't stop the shudder that ran through her body, and the chill that accompanied it made her feel numb. "Thank you," she said, and turned from them to go in search of Cassie.

Inspector Davis caught her and grabbed her arm. "This is a first for you, Anna, and I hope it never happens again. But whether or not it does, understand this: the worst mistake you can make as a commanding officer is to walk around with a load of guilt if one of yours takes a hit. It's not your fault. Do you understand me, Lieutenant?"

She heard him with the small part of her brain that was still taking in facts; the largest part was processing information, what little bit she had, and what she wanted at this moment was first to find the cops who answered the call and found Cassie, and then to get actively in the way of the Mobile Crime Unit, to learn everything they discovered about what happened to Cassie.

"Yes, sir. I understand."

"Is there anything I can do for you, Anna?" Inspector Davis's tone of voice had changed and there was a concern so gentle it made her want to cry.

"What do I tell her parents?" she asked, and almost did cry. That was one of the functions that she abstractly understood to be part of her job. That she should actually need to perform it had never crossed her mind.

"We'll take care of that," the Chief barked.

She nodded her thanks to the Chief and to Inspector Davis, and walked down the corridor to the emergency room. She pushed open the double swinging doors and immediately spied the two uniforms. They were young cops — Casssie's age — one male, one female, and they looked sad, scared, and angry. All cops did when someone got one of their own. She approached them and introduced herself and a little part of her managed a smile at the way they stiffened to attention.

"Please tell me everything you can about what happened to Officer Ali, beginning with how the call came."

She walked them through the story three times until she knew the aspects as well as they: they responded to a shots-fired call at 10:47 p.m. They were three blocks away and arrived in less than two minutes. A man in his underwear and sneakers was running toward them as their patrol car approached. He was yelling that it was a policewoman who was beat up, that he hadn't known that when he first called about hearing the gunshot. The responding officers — their names were Peters and Ianello — followed the man into the alley beside his house. As they ran he told them he'd heard a commotion, which he ignored. Then he heard muffled screams, which subsided. But that prompted him to look out of his bedroom window into the alley below. He didn't see anything, so he returned to the book he was reading. Then he heard a definite scream, followed by a shot, followed by a man's scream, then footsteps running and they were directly under his window. The man then called the police, shoved his feet into his sneakers, grabbed a flashlight from his kitchen pantry, and ran into the alley. He found a woman on the ground, bleeding profusely. She identified herself as a police officer and asked the man to call a number and report an officer down. She made him repeat what she'd told him, the man said, to make sure he got it right. He ran back to the mouth of the alley, toward his house, to make another call to the police when he heard the sirens. He ran to the front of the house just as the first of the squad cars arrived — Peters and Ianello.

Gianna looked from one to the other. Because they didn't know her, all they saw was clear, calm hazel eyes. Because they didn't know her, all they heard was a low, controlled voice, pleasant to the ear. So when she asked, "Did she say anything to you?" and when Peters responded, "She said something like, 'Get Sophie,'" neither of the young officers was prepared for the transformation.

"If she told you who did this to her, you will remember and you will remember exactly what she said, not 'she said something like.' I hope you both understand that." And she left them standing there while she went to talk to the medical staff.

When she found the emergency room charge nurse and introduced herself, there remained no hint of the anger of a moment ago, just the concern of a superior officer for an endangered subordinate. The nurse reiterated what the Chief had said: Cassie was alive, but in grave danger. "She may lose the eye, Lieutenant," the nurse said.

Gianna went to find a phone to call Eric. Her surprise at not finding him at home gave her the momentary shift of focus that she needed. In the time it took for her to call his beeper and wait by the bank of pay phones in the emergency room hallway for him to respond, she took control of herself. She would have to be in control when Eric called, especially since he would not recognize the number, and she'd left only her name and the pay phone number instead of the details of the message because she didn't want him to learn the truth from the tiny screen of the beeper as she had.

"Eric, it's me," she said when she picked up the phone.

"Where are you and what's wrong?"

She felt his tension. "MedStar ER. It's Cassie. Somebody . . . did her. She's not in good shape, Eric."

She was listening to a dial tone.

It was not Cassie she allowed herself to see in the bed, but a victim. She flashed her ID to the uniform stationed at the door, and again at the Mobile Crime Unit technician who stood near the bed watching while another tech took samples from beneath Cassie's nails. When he stood and turned, they recognized each other and his eyebrows shot up in surprise and he let go a low whistle.

"Jesus, Maglione, she one of yours?" He whistled

again. "Fuck. I'm real sorry. What the hell was she working this time of night over near C.U.?"

"She wasn't, Kozlowski. She lives over there."

"Jesus." Kozlowski whistled again. "She looks like a baby, Maglione. How old is she?"

"Twenty-four. You finished yet?" Gianna wasn't in the mood to be civil, though she knew that Kozlowski had come as close as he ever would — or could — to exhibiting the human emotion that was concern for the well-being of another human being. He was without question one of the best evidence techs in the Department. What his eyes didn't see, his cameras did. He was to a crime scene what the forensic pathologist was to a murder victim. But Willie Kozlowski responded to facts, to evidence, not to people.

"Who's working the location, Kozlowski?" Gianna asked.

"Greer, probably, or Anderson. Why? You want me?"

"If I can't have God," she replied with simple honesty.

He chuckled and finished marking and sealing the plastic envelopes into which he'd deposited hairs and fibers and dirt and whatever else was under Cassie's nails, on her clothes, in her hair, on her skin. Then he got out his cameras, one loaded with color film, the other with black and white, and began taking photographs of Cassie — close-ups of her face and her hands and her body showing all the damage, and then of her clothes, torn and blood-stained. And it wasn't until Gianna saw the ripped garments that she wondered whether rape had been a part of this attack, and that's when Cassie ceased being a victim and Gianna had to leave the room.

She collided with the nurse on her way out, and asked her.

"No, Lieutenant, but it's not because they didn't try. That kid put up one hell of a fight. When you find who did it, you'll find pieces missing from his face."

"Good for you, Cassie," Gianna muttered. "When do you take her to surgery?" she asked the nurse.

"They're waiting for us right now. I hope your people are finished," the nurse said, and she gave Gianna's shoulder a gentle squeeze on her way into Cassie's room.

Gianna was headed back down the corridor to the phones to call Mimi when she heard her name called. She looked around to see Eric barreling down the hallway toward her, followed by Lynda Lopez and Bobby Gilliam. Before they asked, she told them everything she knew and then Eric told her that Tim McCreedy and Kenny Chang were already en route to the scene. Gianna told Lynda and Bobby about the two responding officers who needed a brief memory improvement course, and she told Eric to grab Kozlowski when he was finished with Cassie and meet her at the scene. Then she hurried down the hall, through the waiting room crammed with gunshot and stabbing victims, with crying children and pregnant women, with frightened old people, out of the emergency room, and gratefully inhaled the night air, still warm but with the first hint of a cooler undercurrent that signaled the advent of fall.

A siren split the silence and an ambulance screeched out of the circular driveway and headed west.

The automatic doors of the emergency room whooshed open and a middle-aged man pushed a squeaky wheelchair out on to the walkway, its passenger working hard to stifle a groan of pain. Gianna looked down on a tiny, ancient, white haired woman the color of roasted pecans, bundled and huddled within a pink crocheted blanket. The old woman failed to stifle another groan of pain and Gianna winced at the sound of it.

"I'll get the car, Mama, and I'll be right back."

"All right, son," the old woman whispered, the love and gratitude in her voice overriding the pain. A distant siren wailed and grew ever closer and the ancient woman looked up at Gianna and whispered through her pain, "Lord have mercy, there's so much misery in the world."

"Too much," Gianna whispered back but the siren's scream made it impossible for the woman to hear, so Gianna touched the woman's hand, gnarled and twisted like the roots of an old banyan tree, and, trying to close her ears to the sounds of pain, to the songs of the night, she re-entered the hospital because she remembered that she had no car, and while she waited for Eric she called Mimi to tell her that it would be quite some time before she came home.

David Bradley worked for the Bell Atlantic Telephone Company as a line maintenance supervisor.

He was forty-six years old, divorced, the father of three, and had lived in the rented house in the Brookland section of northeast D.C. near Catholic University for three years, since his divorce. No, he did not know the young woman whom he had found beaten up in the alley beneath his bedroom window. Yes, he knew she lived across the street — he'd seen her several times, had exchanged pleasantries with her, had commented to himself what a polite and well-mannered young woman she was. So many of today's young people were not. Yes, he did have some idea why she might have been in the alley: He knew for a fact that she rented garage space from the woman on the next street over and the garage backed onto the alley. She walked through it every night to get home. No, he'd had no idea that she was a police officer until she'd told him so, when she asked him to call and report a police officer down.

Gianna sat on David Bradley's couch in his neat, sparsely furnished living room, drinking a cup of peppermint tea laced with honey which he had insisted would calm her nerves. He was right. She found the tea soothing as she quickly explained to him who she was, who Cassie was, and why the police would most likely be a fixture in his life for some days to come. Then she asked him to tell her what he'd already told to at least three other cops.

She sat back, crossed her legs, and listened intently as Bradley told her exactly what she'd heard earlier from Officers Peters and Ianello. She was grateful for the man's calm, factual recitation, and she didn't speak until he came to the point when he repeated Cassie's words.

"Mr. Bradley, tell me again exactly what Officer Ali said when you and the other officers were with her."

"She said, 'Don't let 'em get to Sophie.' Over and over she said it. Three, maybe four times. 'Don't let 'em get to Sophie.' "

"Did you see anyone else in the alley?"

"No, ma'am. Not a soul. Just her."

Gianna called the Fourth District watch commander and had a car sent to Sophie Gwertzman's house, then she went out into the alley to watch Kozlowski begin the tedious but exacting process of converting bits and pieces of dirt and gravel into evidence.

Gianna sat on the bed. Then she lay down beside the one she always thought of as most like herself. She wanted to hold her but she knew not to touch her. Too much damage. Too much pain. She couldn't even take and hold one of her hands: tubes ran into both arms. So she lay there beside her, listening to the labored breath. She didn't turn her head to see her. She didn't need to look again. The devastating destruction was forever etched in her memory. The left eye that the doctors questioned would ever see again. The bruises on the head and face that signified a brain swollen from the trauma of being kicked repeatedly in the head. She just lay there and listened to the in and out of the breath, listened to assure herself that there was no danger of the breath stopping.

141

X

Since no member of the Hate Crimes Unit had
been home the night before, no one of them minded
that all of them looked like hell. Six pairs of
bloodshot eyes tried to look everywhere but at each
other. Six pairs of lips slurped too hot, too bitter
coffee without a single complaint. Six pairs of hands
fiddled with paper clips or ink pens or crime folders,
just to have something to do with themselves. Finally
Gianna spoke.

"Eric, you handle Cassie today, I'll stay with the

hookers. Maybe they'll let you help with the Mobile Crime stuff and the house-to-house search. Somebody had to see something."

"It was the fuckin' Nazis." Tim's voice was so flat and dead nobody would have recognized it as his had they not been watching his mouth move.

"We don't know who it was, Tim," Gianna said, her own voice void of the tone and tenor that made it so distinctive.

"It was the fuckin' Nazis," he said again. "Can I work with Detective Ashby?" Tim looked at her, dull blue eyes meeting dull hazel ones.

"Yeah. You and Kenny work Cassie with Eric for the day. Lynda, you and Bobby work with me on the Daniel Boone thing. Everybody back here at five-thirty sharp."

When Mimi identified herself, Carolyn King opened the door wide and invited her inside. The first thing Mimi saw when she stepped into the homey, comfortable living room was a framed photo-graph — the high school graduation photograph — of the woman she knew as Shelley Kelley. The woman Carolyn King knew as her daughter, Sandra Ann King.

"I'm very sorry about what happened to your daughter, Mrs. King," Mimi said, crossing to stand before the mantel.

"She was getting ready to quit. Did you know that? She was going to leave all that."

The woman sighed heavily. Close scrutiny of her

face indicated that she was not old — Mimi would guess that she was barely fifty — yet the weight of her sadness made her feel at least twice that.

"She had stopped doing drugs and she was eating right. Even got me to stop eating red meat. My blood pressure dropped so fast it scared the doctor."

Carolyn King stood and paced the small room, rubbing her hands together as if trying to warm them. Mimi studied her, trying to understand who she was, for she was too young to fit the stereotype she resembled — that of a grandmother scarred by the weight of generations of injustice — yet the fatigue that emanated from her was palpable, as were the sorrow and the sadness which distorted her underlying handsomeness.

"And she was putting money in the bank. She had money, you see, because she wasn't buying those drugs any more. She was saving to go to computer school . . "

The woman stopped talking. It seemed that she just ran out of words. Mimi found the woman's pain almost too much to bear.

"Was Sandra your only child, Mrs. King?" Mimi asked, picking up the framed photograph.

"She was my only girl. And I had so much hope for her." And Carolyn King began to cry softly as she told Mimi how it happened that at age fifty she'd buried two husbands, three sons and a daughter. The first husband, whom she married when both were just nineteen years old, came back from Viet Nam literally in pieces, in a body bag. The son of that marriage, born while his father was in Southeast Asia and who never saw his father, drowned in a boating accident as a teenager. The second husband and one son died in a car crash ten years ago. The remaining son died from a drug overdose. And now Sandra. "All I have left is Sandra's baby and I'm scared to death I might do something to hurt her."

"Why would you think that?" Mimi said tightly.

"Look what happened to all the others. It must be something I'm doing to make them all die."

The woman's words, spoken so simply and so devoid of emotion, devastated Mimi. She could think of nothing to say; and, in truth, the woman expected no response. So Mimi said what she'd come to say. "Your daughter wanted to tell me something, Mrs. King, did you know that?"

"I knew it. And I knew she wanted some money from you."

Mimi ducked dealing with that issue. "I think if I could find out what she wanted to tell me, I could find out who killed her."

"You think it had something to do with those boys?"

"What boys?"

"Sandra said there was some boys who had a club and they had to kill one of the girls to get in the club."

The buzzing inside Mimi's head was so loud she couldn't think for a moment, because it was competing with the guilt that was washing over her in waves. Why the hell hadn't she just paid Shelley — Sandra — for the story? Why hadn't she just given her the money? The girl would be alive today.

"Did she know the boys, Mrs. King?"

"Oh, no. They weren't from around here. These were white boys, Sandra said, rich ones. From the suburbs."

* * * * *

Gianna moved through the early part of the day on automatic pilot. Every hour she called the hospital for an update on Cassie, and every hour she was told that Cassie remained in a coma, that the swelling in her brain still constituted a grave danger. At noon, she had lunch with the Chief in his office. She told him about Cassie's unchanged condition; then she told him about the newest murder and about the new murder count and the black Jeep registered to the Utah Congressman, and he cursed for a full minute without stopping and without once repeating himself. He told her to keep Tony Watkins and Alice Long and use them however she needed them and for as long as she needed them.

And then he told her that Sophie Gwertzman had committed suicide when she heard what happened to Cassie Ali. And it was Gianna's turn to curse, though not for as long nor nearly as proficiently as the Chief.

After their meeting, she paid a quick visit to the hospital and got a full briefing from the doctor who'd just completed a check of Cassie, who was still comatose but holding her own.

When she returned to the Think Tank shortly after two, Tony and Alice were waiting for her, and she required another adjustment period, for today they were dressed in regular street clothes.

"We heard about your Officer Ali, Lieutenant," Alice said, "and if there's anything we can do . . "

"There is," Gianna said quickly, offering them both what passed for a smile these days, and taking a seat opposite them at the table. But before she could tell them what she wanted, the door opened and a huge box appeared in the doorway, followed by an officer in uniform, such a rarity for the Think Tank that she wondered whether he'd come to the wrong place.

"You Lieutenant Maglione?" he asked in her general direction.

"What's all this?" She pointed to the box that he'd dropped heavily onto the floor and which was loaded with files.

"That's the stuff you asked for."

"What stuff who asked for?" she said frowning.

"From WASIS. Didn't you request a run on a black Jeep —"

"Good God!" Gianna jumped up from the chair and rushed across the room to the officer and the bulging box. He took a step backward, his hand on the doorknob. "All this from one license check?"

"And this isn't all of it. You only got a level eight access. You need a ten to get the rest of it. Sign here," he said, giving her a form and a pen. She signed, he tore off the back copy of the form, gave it to her, saluted, and left.

Before she could do or say anything, Tony crossed the room, scooped up the box, and hauled it to the table where he stood peering into it warily, as if expecting something from within to attack. "*This* is the file on the black Jeep Wrangler?"

Tony couldn't keep the disbelief out of his voice, and Gianna didn't blame him. She could hardly believe it herself. What the hell had they all just stepped in? This thing had a bad smell to it.

"I assume no mistake was made on the license number?"

"You assume one hundred percent correctly, Lieutenant." Alice's soft, Southern voice had an edge to it that was new to Gianna, and her gaze was fixed steadily on the box of files. "And you know somethin'? This doesn't surprise me. All those boys in that car, just ridin' around night after night. Why? Never pickin' up a woman? Uh uh," Alice said, shaking her head in a way that sharply and painfully reminded Gianna of Cassie's way of responding when the shit was piling up too high.

"Well, let's see what we've got," Gianna said, putting on her reading glasses to study the index of what was in the files. She saw that they were arranged by date. One by one, she removed them as she checked to make certain that they corresponded to the index. Then she apportioned them among the three of them and they grouped themselves around the table to begin the process of building what Gianna believed could be the foundation of the case against the killer — and now it certainly seemed that it would be killers — of nine women.

They were deeply engrossed in the files when Lynda and Bobby returned. They stopped short at the sight of the two strangers working at the table with Gianna. She introduced Tony and Alice and explained the piles of documents and what they were doing, and watched as the four young cops sized up each other, Lynda and Bobby definitely in a territorial stance, Tony and Alice holding their own, but clearly the interlopers. She restored the calm and unruffled the feathers by involving Lynda and Bobby in the work, and the five of them worked in silence until Eric returned with Tim and Kenny precisely at five-thirty. She made the introductions of Alice and

Tony again, and again explained the mass of documents. But with Eric's return, what she wanted was an update on the Cassie investigation.

Eric quickly and succinctly walked her through the work the lab had done in record time, primarily because everybody in the lab wanted to get rid of Tim as soon as possible. Eric said Tim's ominous presence made everybody wish he were being a screaming queen again instead of the cold, silent avenger that he'd become.

Tony and Alice stared at Tim, looking for signs that he was a screaming queen, then gazed at Eric looking for signs that perhaps he was joking. They shrugged at each other and listened as Eric continued. According to the lab reports, Cassie had significant samples of skin, hair and blood under her nails from at least two different sources. And there were two different types of blood on her clothes, other than her own. There was also significant blood in the alley . . .

"She shot one of the bastards," Tim said coldly, which caused Bobby to stand and silently raise a clenched fist.

"Way to go, Cassie," Lynda said almost reverently.

The trail of blood, Eric continued, led down the alley, through a yard, and into the next street where it stopped in the grass at the curb, suggesting that the victim had gotten into a car parked there.

"Did anybody see anything?" Gianna asked.

Eric's jaw tightened. "A woman who was washing her dishes saw two white males . . ."

"I told you, Lieutenant, it was the fuckin' Nazis," Tim said.

149

"Don't interrupt me again, Tim," Eric said calmly, and continued, ". . . run through the alley behind her house. One seemed to be supporting the other, almost carrying him, were her words. They both wore dark or black clothes — shirts and pants — and one wore a cap and the other had short hair. She would not recognize them again. It was too dark." Eric snapped his notebook shut.

"So everything points to there being two of them?"

"So far, Anna."

"And Cassie marked both of them . . ."

"The CID guys have our list of known Nazis, neo-Nazis, Aryan Nationites, skin heads, white supremacists — all the ones we know about, they know about, and they're running them to ground. Believe me, if they spot one of those punks with so much as a razor burn, they'll haul his ass in." Eric sighed and rubbed his hand back and forth against the stubble of growth on his face.

Gianna watched him, thinking idly that men's beards often grew in a different color from their hair.

"All right," she said abruptly. "Let me bring you up to speed on the hooker thing . . ."

"But what about Cassie?" Tim asked plaintively. "Is that all we're gonna do?"

"That's all we can do, Tim. It's not our case."

"*Not our case?*" Tim jumped up with a force that sent his chair skidding out behind him. "Cassie is *ours*! Doesn't that make it our case?"

Gianna saw that he was close to tears. She stood, went and got his chair and brought it back to the table. "Sit down, Tim." She pointedly waited until he sat before she continued. Allowing team members to

150

express their emotions was one thing. Allowing them to get out of control was quite another.

"Every one of us is thrown out of whack by what happened to Cassie. But we investigate hate crimes, not assaults on police officers. Now, everybody cut us some slack today — that's why the lab guys put up with your evil ass all day, Tim — because they all know how we feel. Now we have to cut them some slack by staying clear so they can do their jobs. We have our own work to do and I expect you — all of you — to do that work. Am I clear?"

She looked around the table and met and held everybody's eyes, including Tony's and Alice's, until she got a "Yes, Ma'am" or a "Yes, Boss," from each of them. Then she stood, walked to stand in front of the blackboard and the map, and told them what was in the WASIS file produced by the license plate of one black Jeep Wrangler.

The vehicle was registered to Utah Congressman Earl Allyne but belonged to his son, Errol Allyne, a twenty-year-old junior at the University of Virginia, who had been dismisssed the previous year from the U.S. Naval Academy in Annapolis. "Errol and three of his nearest and dearest — Todd Haldane, Jerome Wilson and Clarke Andrews — have been arrested a total of twelve times, individually and collectively, on a variety of charges ranging from drunk driving to attempted rape. Eight of the twelve incidents involve assaults on women. In every one of those cases, the charges were dropped by the complainant. Two of the incidents involve the possession of a controlled substance, specifically cocaine, and the others are destruction of property resulting from drunk and disorderly. Haldane, Wilson, and Andrews are the sons, respectively, of a United States Senator, a Foreign Service officer, and an Army brigadier general who is assigned to the Joint Chiefs of Staff. All of the incidents involving Allyne, Haldane, Wilson, and Andrews occurred in the Virginia and Maryland suburbs, specifically in McLean and Fairfax in Virginia, and in Bethesda and Gaithersburg in Maryland. All of the incidents occurred within the last three years."

Gianna had been pacing slowly back and forth in front of the blackboard. She stopped and faced them. "I need a higher clearance to access the rest of this file. But I'll bet I know what's in it: these guys' juvenile records." She paced some more. "These boys didn't turn bad on the morning of their eighteenth birthdays."

What she thought but didn't say was that if these boys had been born poor or Black or Hispanic, they'd be in a jail by now, not transferring from one prestigious university to another. She struggled to control the disgust she felt for their fathers, who had peddled a lot of influence and spread around a lot of money to keep their sons out of jail. And if she didn't turn up more than the circumstantial evidence she had so far, there would be nothing she could do to change that pattern.

She gave Tony and Alice the night off and ordered her Team to get a good night's sleep as well, warning them that another such opportunity would not present itself in the near future. She called the Chief and requested, and immediately received, a level ten clearance to access the rest of the WASIS file, which was promised to her the following day.

Then she drove across town to the Washington

Hospital Center to see Cassie and to meet her parents, and was surprised at how relieved she was at the warmth of their greeting, before she identified the source of the relief: she had been afraid that the Alis would blame her for what happened to their daughter. She studied them, noting which of her traits Cassie had inherited from which parent. Cassie was the spitting image of the petite, pretty, dark brown woman who was her mother; but where Cassie was always angry about something, her mother looked as if she'd never been angry in her life. She was the most peaceful-seeming person Gianna had ever seen. Cassie's nonstop energy came from her father. He was half a foot taller than his wife, wiry and strong-looking, and though he stood perfectly still at the foot of Cassie's bed, Gianna could feel the energy coursing through him. He clenched and unclenched his hands and Gianna imagined that the man was thinking what he'd do if he could get his hands on the men who'd hurt his little girl.

They quietly left the room and Gianna stood beside the bed looking down on the battered face, looking for the beauty she knew was there but obscured by the destruction, looking for some sign of the sparkling intelligence that still lived, she was certain, somewhere within the swollen, damaged brain. What she sought she could not find. But what she certainly knew still existed was the fighting spirit that endeared Cassandra Ali to her heart. She knew the spirit was still there because the girl now was breathing evenly, deeply, without the assistance of a respirator. Her one good eye, the right one, fluttered gently behind the closed lid. Cassandra Ali was still there. Gianna was certain of it.

* * * * *

Mimi's car was in the parking lot when Gianna arrived at the gym, so she rushed in, quickly changed into her workout clothes, and hurried into the spacious room. The music was pumping and Gianna quickly got caught up in the energy of the place. She spied Mimi running on the treadmill and, stopping to chat briefly with a couple of women, and waving to several others, she worked her way across the floor and came up unnoticed behind Mimi.

"I love it when you sweat," she said, just loud enough for Mimi to hear, and she turned and grinned.

"Prove it," she challenged, not breaking her stride.

"Your place or mine?" Gianna asked, starting the treadmill next to Mimi's, setting the speed at maximum, and starting to run.

"Yours," Mimi answered, and they ran in step for the next half hour, each lost in her own thoughts, thoughts that included the other as well as those portions of their day that had caused them pain and frustration and sadness.

Mimi preferred to work her upper body with free weights when she was stressed, and Gianna preferred to work the machines, so their workout was separate except for the leg machines. They alternated sets of leg presses and curls, squats, and lunges, and then separated again when Gianna opted for standing calf raises while Mimi preferred seated ones. They came together again for abdominal work, each doing a hundred crunches, cross crunches, and leg lifts, and finishing with long, slow stretches. They took a long steam, during which neither of them spoke very much except to agree that Mimi would stop and pick up Chinese food for herself and pizza for Gianna, and meet Gianna at her place.

They ate in bed, watching a video that should have been returned a week ago, still not talking very much but each very much feeling the presence of the other. Though they rarely drank during the week, Gianna had a beer and Mimi a glass of wine.

Finally, full and relaxed, Mimi gathered Gianna in her arms.

"How's Cassie?"

"Still in a coma. I saw her before coming to the gym. I think . . . I know it sounds crazy, but I think she's going to pull out of it. Soon."

"Doesn't sound crazy at all." Mimi rubbed Gianna's neck and shoulders, trying to work out some of the tension knotted there.

"How are the others taking it?"

Gianna sighed. "About like you'd expect. Except Tim."

"The good-looking one? What's he doing?"

"Coming apart at the seams. He lost it this afternoon. He and Cassie are very close."

"They're the only gay ones, right?"

"Yeah, but their bond is deeper than that. Despite Tim's display of outrageousness and Cassie's cutting cynicism, they're both such idealists. They became cops to make the world a better place. And it really gets to them that most days the bad guys win." Gianna sighed, reached for her beer, and took a long pull. "They're like you in that regard."

Mimi arched her eyebrows and her voice. "Like moi? And whatever do you mean by that, Lieutenant, Ma'am?"

"I mean that they don't see shades of gray. For them — for you — things are either right or they're wrong. All the time. Not maybe right today and maybe not so right tomorrow."

"Is that a bad thing, Gianna?"

"No. Just sometimes a very painful thing."

Mimi thought of Carolyn King and the granddaughter she was afraid would die, too. She thought of Shelley and Starry and the other women who were dead because, if Carolyn King was correct, some rich kids used them for target practice. She felt the part of her that didn't want to believe such a thing was possible. She felt the part of her that wanted to talk to Gianna about it. Then she felt the part of her that wanted to make things right for Carolyn King and for her daughter and for her daughter's daughter.

Gianna felt her thinking and feeling and turned over to face her. She leaned on her elbows, looking into Mimi's eyes, probing, searching, questioning. Mimi kissed her, lightly, gently. She didn't want to talk because she didn't know what to say, so she changed the subject.

"I thought you were going to make me sweat."

And Gianna, with a seriousness and an intensity and a dedication to purpose that were breathtaking, made good on her promise.

* * * * *

Adrienne Lightfoot would not even allow Mimi to enter the Washington Center for Spiritual Awareness. She was gracious and polite and even charming as she kept Mimi on the outside of the front door. And she was implacable in her refusal to talk to Mimi about Sandra, or to allow Mimi to talk to her about what Carolyn King said Sandra told her.

"Miss Lightfoot, those women are in danger," Mimi said to the space in the door where Adrienne Lightfoot stood.

"They are most likely more aware than you of that fact, Miss Patterson," Adrienne Lightfoot said quite calmly, and closed the door.

Sylvia was considerably more receptive — she let Mimi in and gave her a cup of tea — though no more encouraging.

"But what do you want me to do, Mimi? Being threatened is a part of those women's daily lives. They won't stop working because of threats."

"Not threats, Sylvia, murder." Mimi was trying to remain calm but was losing patience. "Don't they believe that Sandra and the others are really dead?"

"They believe it, Mimi," Sylvia said with a trace of weariness. "They just don't believe that it could happen to them."

Mimi drove downtown mumbling and muttering to herself. "It can't happen to me." The swan song of every victim everywhere. Bad things happen to other people. Muggings. Rape. AIDS. *I can do whatever I want as long as I'm careful because bad things happen to other people.*

So engrossed was she in her mental tirade with

herself that she had to swerve to miss hitting a taxi that abruptly crossed into her lane en route to pick up a passenger at the curb. Mimi cursed and honked her horn, then had to make herself slow down and calm down. She searched herself for the cause of her out-of-sorts feeling and was surprised when she discovered the reason: Ever since she had left Carolyn King's house, her efforts and concerns had not been about her story, but about the people involved. She hadn't stood there talking to Adrienne Lightfoot through a crack in a door for a story, she had done it for the women who sell their bodies on the street. That was the same reason she'd dropped in on Sylvia, and it was for a related reason that she was now on her way to Beverly's new office, although she hadn't known that was where she was going until that very moment.

The Midtown Psychotherapy Associates occupied all three floors of a beautifully restored townhouse in a still shitty part of D.C. that was close enough to the gentrified part of LeDroit Park to hold out hope for better days to come. True, the campus of Howard University was a few blocks to the east, and the new city government building was several blocks to the north, but Bev's building stood right smack in the middle of raging urban blight. The whole damn block needed psychotherapy.

Mimi walked up the steps and tried to open the locked door. Frowning, she looked all around, then up and into the blinking eye of a security camera. Then she found the buzzer she needed to press to gain entry, and felt immediately better. At least the place was secure. At least Bev was safe here.

"Your name and appointment time, please," said a voice from a speaker Mimi didn't see.

"I don't have an appointment, but I'd like to see Beverly Connors if she's available. My name is Montgomery Patterson."

"One moment, please," said the invisible voice, and Mimi studied the massive oak door and the heavily barred windows while she waited, feeling better about the place.

In just a few seconds a buzzer sounded and Mimi pushed open the heavy door which brought her into a foyer only to encounter another, metal, door through which she was buzzed, finally, into a bright, warm reception area that was packed with people — mostly young women and school-aged children — but there were two men, one of whom sat holding the hand of a terrified-looking boy; several sullen teenagers; and three women who looked at least sixty. Mimi was relieved to see them. It made her feel not so foolish for coming. And when, half an hour later, she was talking to Beverly in her office, she definitely felt much better than foolish.

"The woman hasn't had a breakdown only because she hasn't had time," Bev said sadly. Mimi had told her all about Carolyn King's life, and her comment that she was afraid she'd do something to hurt Sandra's daughter. "I remember my mother and her friends saying that as a joke, as they wondered at the luxury of white women seeing shrinks, and sending their children for therapy. My mother would laugh and shake her head and say, 'Who in the world has time to have a nervous breakdown? I've got a husband and three children to take care of. Who'd cook dinner and do the laundry?'"

"So, how do I get her to come see you?" Mimi asked.

"I think you put it to her directly: If you want to talk to somebody, Mrs. King, these people specialize in Black families, especially women and children. She can only call or not call. Either way, Mimi, you've just done a wonderful thing. Don't tell me you're becoming a human being."

Mimi was still smarting about the human being crack when she walked into the newsroom. She dropped her purse and jacket at her desk and crossed the huge, noisy area to the wall of offices at the rear of the room where the editors lived. She passed Tyler's desk, caught his eye and gave him a thumbs up, as she went in search of her boss-in-name-only, the special projects editor. Mimi didn't like him, didn't respect him, and didn't want to work for him. But she'd have to be careful how she played her cards. Her last two major stories she'd worked for Tyler, politically dangerous ground for her boss, who was known as a turf fighter.

She knocked on his door and went in. As usual, he was reading some boring government report. His idea of a good book was the federal budget. His idea of a good story was anything that involved a government report. Which was why he kept funneling immigration reports to her. She thought, as she did every time she saw him, how dumb he looked. For some reason, he dressed like a Connecticut Avenue lawyer, not like a journalist. He wore Brooks Brothers suits and wing tip shoes and starched shirts and his Phi Beta Kappa key and chain, and the pungent odor of expensive Cuban cigars always hovered about him, though Mimi had never seen him smoke. Maybe he wore his father's clothes...

"Got a minute?"

"Sure." He waved her into a chair. "What's up?"

"Five hookers, not four, all killed by a six-inch hunting knife expertly thrown from a passing vehicle. The Daniel Boone murders, the cops are calling them."

She sat, watching and waiting, as he digested what she'd just told him. She knew he wondered how she found out, that he was attempting to calculate how long it would take for her to work the story, and that he was trying to figure whether his boss, the senior editor, would rather read about Salvadoreans without green cards or some Daniel Boone murders.

But out of his mouth came what was really on his mind. "That's a city desk story, Patterson. The third one in a row. You forget who you work for?" He grinned, showing small, neat teeth, but the smile never reached his eyes. This guy would bag her the first chance he got.

She shrugged nonchalantly. "Give the story to a city desk reporter if you want."

"Do your information sources come with the story?"

"Not in this life." She answered so coldly that he visibly winced.

He picked up the phone and punched four digits. She knew without looking that he'd called Tyler.

161

"Can you come in for a moment, please?" The half smile still raised the corners of his mouth. He didn't speak to her during the few seconds before the knock came and Tyler sauntered in.

"Tell him what you just told me. That is if you haven't already told him."

"She's already told me nothing." Mimi loved it when Tyler bristled. "But I'm listening," he said, turning his attention not only to Mimi but distinctly away from the scowling presence behind the desk.

So Mimi told him in detail what she knew, including a veiled reference to an organized group of well-to-do young men who killed women as part of some kind of initiation rite.

Tyler whistled. "That's like that Billionaire Boys Club business out in, where was it, California? And wasn't there something like that in New York?"

"You mean that thing in Central Park?"

"Yeah, and come to think of it, there was another group of boys in California, high school boys, passed young girls around for sex."

They both became aware at the same time that their editor not only didn't know what they were talking about, he didn't care. He'd already returned to his government report. Mimi wondered for a moment how the fool kept his job before she remembered his Ivy League credentials and the similar credentials of the decision makers at the paper, and she knew that he'd be around for a while.

Gianna had spent the better part of the last hour on the phone with an investigator in the Fairfax

County police department, who was confirming her worst suspicions about Errol Allyne and his friends. The file that she had compiled on them in the past few days was more than a little disturbing. Not only did it reflect a pattern of juvenile delinquency that had turned to adult criminality, but throughout there was evidence of parental tolerance at an unbelievable level. In addition to the juvenile records of the four boys, which Gianna had suspected was the reason she needed a top clearance to access the entire case file, there was also the report of an assault on a police officer by the father of one of the boys, the reason why Gianna was talking to the Fairfax County cop: Sergeant Marx was the one assaulted, and General Jefferson Davis Andrews, father of Clarke Andrews, had done the assaulting.

"The man is a monster!" exclaimed Sergeant Marx, and he recalled for Gianna events that led to his altercation with General Andrews.

He was one of three cars that responded to a call in an exclusive section of inherently exclusive McLean, Virginia. They found the remains of what had been a wild party at the home of a girl whose parents were out of town. Only the girl remained, and she had been gang raped and then punched and slapped and kicked in what appeared to be a ritualistic fashion.

"What do you mean, ritualistic fashion?" Gianna asked.

"Just that, Lieutanant. Three boys raped her, then took turns beating her. Each one, egged on by the others, beat her. The boys were sixteen at the time. The girl was fourteen."

Gianna felt sick to her stomach. She didn't want

to hear any more. But Sergeant Marx continued to talk, and she understood that he needed to tell her because although the incident had occurred more than four years ago, the horror of it had not subsided for him, and neither had his anger. The girl identified the boys and told police where they lived: one of them, Clarke Andrews, right around the corner. Calling for back-up, Marx and his partner had rushed immediately to the Andrews home, wanting to prevent the boys from destroying any evidence of the attack. Though there obviously were people in the house, the bell went unanswered for several minutes. Finally the door was opened and the officers identified themselves and asked permission to enter. They were met by a stream of profanity from the man they later learned was General Andrews.

"My partner at the time was a female officer," related Marx, "and she cautioned Andrews that his words and manner could be construed to be threatening. He called her a castrating bitch and threw a punch at her. I couldn't believe it! She reacted before I did and tried to get him in a choke-hold. But this guy is some kind of martial arts expert. It took both of us to subdue him, and I don't mind telling you I gave him a hard knee to the nuts."

Gianna managed a small grin at the satisfaction she heard in his voice. He quickly wrapped up the rest of the story: the back-up units arrived and found five boys barricaded in an upstairs bedroom. Three of them had cuts and lacerations about the face; the other two had been at the party but, it turned out, had been too drunk to participate in the rape.

Downstairs in the basement, a load of clothes was in the washing machine — the evidence going cleanly down the drain. And in a small bedroom in the basement was a woman, the wife of the General and the mother of Clarke, so drunk and disoriented that she literally didn't know who or where she was. The General and the boys were arrested and the washing machine confiscated. Three days later, the girl dropped all charges against the boys. The Commonwealth's Attorney tried to bring a case but the girl's parents refused to allow her to cooperate. The police department agreed to drop its assault charges against General Andrews in exchange for his apology, over the objections of both Marx and his partner.

"Lieutenant, I, for one, would be eternally grateful if you could nail those little fuckers once and for all," Marx said with vehemence. "People like them make a mockery of people like you and me."

Gianna agreed with him and was thanking him for his cooperation when he added a final comment — the impression that still remained most vividly in his mind about the incident. Gianna couldn't imagine that there could be more, and was completely unprepared for what he said.

"Those five red cars lined up in front of that house. Looked like a fucking car dealership."

"Sergeant . . . I'm sorry. I don't understand. What five red cars?"

"I didn't tell you? All those boys in that club of theirs drove the same make and color of car. That year it was red Trans Ams. You know how much those things cost?"

Gianna gratefully concluded the phone call with

Sergeant Marx. Sometime toward the end of it, she'd developed an odd detachment from the entire matter and now she wondered about it.

She began her habitual pacing about the Think Tank, relieved to have the space to herself for a while. Certainly the horrible images painted by Marx were disturbing. But what troubled her was more, deeper somehow . . . Cassie. It was Cassie, specifically, and the brutalization of women generally, that disturbed her inner core. That and the fact that such brutality seemed to have moved out of the relative privacy — and secrecy — of domesticity, into the realm of sport, of group activity for boys and young men. She felt the anger rise within her as she thought of the two who had brutalized Cassie. Then she had another thought, her own final image of the scene painted by Sergeant Marx, and it wasn't of five red sports cars but of a sad, lonely, brutalized woman living in the basement of her own home, afraid, almost certainly, of the man she called husband, and probably of the child she'd risked her life to bring to earth. In that moment, Gianna wanted nothing more than to smash her fist into the collective faces of the perpetuators of such hatred.

Cassie had awakened from her coma. Gianna arrived at the hospital first, and rushed into the room filled with brightly colored, exotic flowers and green houseplants of every description, and balloons that said Get Well Soon and I Love You and a silly assortment of stuffed animals and boxes of Cassie's favorite chocolates. But the real brightness of the

166

room was the joy brought by Cassie's awakening. Gianna gratefully received a warm embrace from both of the girl's parents who then gracefully left the room.

Gianna sat on the side of the bed and took one of Cassie's hands into her own and held it, tightly. Tears fell from the girl's one eye, the one not bandaged, the other one's destruction hidden from view. Gianna wiped away the tears and took the girl gently into her arms.

"Everything will be just fine, Cassie." Gianna held her for a long time, until the tears and the body-wracking sobs ceased and it felt as if she'd fallen asleep. Then she carefully placed her back down in the bed, arranged the pillow and the blankets, and went into the bathroom to get a cloth to bathe her face.

Eric arrived. "She's awake, right?" he asked with a worried look when he saw that Cassie was asleep.

"Out of the coma, yes. But Eric, I don't think she knows what happened to her." And she didn't need to say the rest: That without her positive identification, it would be difficult if not impossible to bring her attackers to justice, especially since there was no eyewitness.

"Damn!" Eric said. "You think it will be permanent?"

The doctor, who briskly entered the room at that moment, confirmed Gianna's suspicion and answered Eric's question. There was no way to tell how extensive Cassie's memory loss ultimately would be, or how permanent. She explained that in cases of severe trauma to the brain, the victim frequently remembered everything up to the few moments before the traumatic event, and selectively thereafter. For example, the doctor said, Cassie remembered nothing between parking her car in the garage near her home, and waking up in the hospital looking at her parents. She really does not, the doctor explained, understand why she is in so much pain.

"Does she know about her eye, Doctor?"

"Not yet," the doctor replied gently. "Do you want to be present when we tell her?"

Gianna sighed deeply. "Do I want to? No. Will I? Yes. But what about her parents?"

"The mother doesn't think she'd be able to tell her and the father is wavering. So I thought that you, as her commanding officer —"

"When?" Gianna asked, cutting off the explanation. If she was going to do it, it didn't really matter why.

"Let's give her another thirty-six to forty-eight hours to stabilize," the doctor advised.

Gianna gave the doctor her card and promised to be available whenever she was needed.

They watched the doctor's departing back, all crisp, white efficiency, and Gianna had to release her irritation with the woman as she acknowledged the similarity of their jobs. The doctor had responded exactly as Gianna did when she had to question witnesses or victims: with calm, unwavering, unemotional efficiency. The doctor was good at her job and Gianna appreciated it. Eric, however, had reached no such place of acceptance.

"This shit is really getting on my nerves," he snarled. "I'm fuckin' sick and tired of hoodlum sons of bitches thinking they can do any goddamn thing they please and get away with it!"

"Well, pal, you ain't heard nothin' yet. Just listen to this," Gianna said without a trace of sympathy in her voice, as she told him what she'd learned from Sergeant Marx of the Fairfax County police.

XI

Mimi hated it when the phone rang in the middle of the night. She'd experimented over the years with having a listed phone number so sources could call her at home when necessary. But then she began to receive more and more crank calls, so she unlisted the number again. As a result, her phone seldom rang past eleven or eleven-thirty at night — her friends knew better. She opened one eye and stared numbly at the red digital read-out. Just past one in the morning.

"Hello," she growled into the phone, picking it up on its third ring.

"Is that you, Newspaper Lady?" came a shaky, frightened voice. There was so much fear in the voice that Mimi knew it was Baby only because no one else called her Newspaper Lady.

"What's the trouble, Baby?"

"They killed another girl and I saw 'em! They threw this knife at her and killed her and I saw 'em! What should I do?"

"Tell me where you are, Baby." Mimi had switched on the light and grabbed the pen and pad she always kept on the table beside her bed. She wrote down an address just west of Thomas Circle, where she'd first met Baby, and the explicit instructions Baby was giving her: there was a one-way alley that ran beside a Methodist Church on the east side of Twelfth Street. Enter the alley going the wrong way — Baby was adamant on that point — and drive slowly through to the opposite end and Baby would appear.

"What kinda car you got, Newspaper Lady?"

"A red Karmann Ghia," Mimi responded without thinking.

"A red *what*?" Baby challenged, in her almost normal tone of voice. "What the hell kinda car is that?"

"If you see a red convertible come through the alley and you don't know what kind of car it is, assume it's me," Mimi snapped, and slammed down the phone.

She dressed in record time, grabbed her tape recorder, notepad and pen, and, one foot out the door of her bedroom, had a thought that sent her scurrying back to the closet, from which she grabbed a nylon windbreaker, a pair of jeans, and a baseball cap.

Eva Mae Harris was a licensed practical nurse. She'd worked for twenty-six years at D.C. General Hospital but had grown weary of the back-breaking, unrewarding work. With her last child out of the house, she'd decided to retire from the hospital and begin private duty nursing. It didn't pay as well and there were no benefits, but with a full pension and no children to feed, the money was enough. Besides, she had Fred's pension check, too.

Eva Mae took care of a woman in Georgetown, a stroke victim. She was supposed to get off duty at eleven-thirty, when the woman's son was due home. But the boy never returned home on time. Treated Eva Mae like she was the maid, like she would stay there until he decided to come home, whenever that was. And because Eva Mae was a good nurse, she did always stay. Tonight the boy stumbled in the door at half past midnight, making Eva Mae more grateful than she already was that neither of her children had ever given her a moment's trouble, despite the fact that they were raised in what some people considered the ghetto, and not in ritzy Georgetown. And so it was that Eva Mae Harris arrived home at almost one-fifteen in the morning to find a prostitute on her front steps, a big knife sticking out of her chest. Ever the nurse, Eva Mae felt for the carotid artery in the woman's neck and determined that she was dead, though she hadn't been for long; she was still quite warm. Then she said a quick prayer for the woman's soul, stepped over her body, went into the house, and called the police.

Mimi turned left on Twelfth Street and crawled down the block until she saw the Grace Methodist Church. She saw the alley beside the church, and she saw the one-way arrow pointing out. Mimi made the illegal turn into the alley, following Baby's instructions, and crept slowly forward into the darkness. She passed the church, crossed an intersecting alley, and was approaching the back of a grocery store when she saw a shadow move. A wave of apprehension shot through her. She had no damn business creeping through some alley in the middle of the night in one of the most dangerous neighborhoods in the city! The shadow loomed larger and Mimi saw Baby step from a concealed doorway. Mimi reached over and unlocked the car door so that it was open when the car drew abreast of Baby, who scampered in, slammed the door, and yelled at Mimi, "Let's get the fuck outta here!"

Mimi put the car in gear and roared through the alley out onto Eleventh Street. Fear replaced by adrenaline, she was trying to convince Baby to show her where the dead woman was and Baby was steadfastly refusing. Suddenly, there was the combined wail of half a dozen sirens and within seconds, police cruisers and ambulances were converging from every direction. Mimi looked around for Gianna's car, assuming that all the activity had to do with what Baby had witnessed less than an hour earlier. Instead of heeding Baby's exhortations to get the hell out of the area, Mimi followed the ambulance. Baby threatened to get out of the car and take a taxi home and Mimi, making a choice, turned a corner and left all the activity behind. She knew where to find the cops. She did not know where to find Baby.

Gianna picked up her phone in the middle of the second ring and sounded wide awake, even though it was two o'clock in the morning. She wrote down the address of the house where the hooker with the knife in her chest had died and cursed herself for not following her impulse to move Tony and Alice to a different location. She stood in the steaming shower a couple of minutes longer than usual because she was, she realized, exhausted. She didn't remember the last night she'd had more than five hours sleep. And at this rate . . .

Mimi was surprised, though pleased, that Baby not only didn't balk at changing into the jacket and jeans that Mimi offered her, but praised Mimi for being smart enough to consider that Baby would require a change of clothes, given the circumstances and the time of morning. Mimi marveled at the ease and speed with which Baby effected the change in the front seat of the tiny car — she shimmied out of the skin-tight body suit and into the jeans in a matter of seconds, but not before Mimi noticed how rail-thin she was. Baby kept on her tank top and added Mimi's jacket, zipping it all the way up. Finally she yanked off the voluminous platinum wig to reveal the close-cut Afro and again Mimi took note of the fact that this woman was little more than a child. And tonight, a frightened child. She popped the baseball cap backwards on her head and turned to Mimi.

"So what kinda car did you say this was?"

"A Karmann Ghia. That's a Volkswagen."

"Bullshit," drawled Baby. "I ain't ever seen no Volkswagen that looked like this car."

"That's because they stopped making it before you were born," Mimi snapped at her. "Now stop maligning my car."

"What's maligning mean?" Baby asked in that guileless tone.

"Means derogatory," Mimi said and caught herself in time to try to fix the error. "Means negative, it means saying bad things."

"I didn't say nothin' maligning about your car. I just said I hadn't never seen one like it." She said it smugly, pleased with her casual use of a new word.

"And you won't see any more like it. It's very rare."

"Does that mean it's worth a lot of money?"

"I've been offered a lot of money for it," Mimi boasted.

"So, why don't you sell it and buy a nice car?"

"Baby, *that's* maligning," Mimi said wearily, pulling up to a parking meter in front of the Connecticut Avenue Diner.

Baby ordered waffles, sausage, eggs, orange juice

and milk. Mimi asked for coffee and returned with defiance the look she got from across the table. She was damned if she'd justify her dietary habits to a smart-mouthed nineteen-year-old who had the temerity to malign her prized classic automobile.

"Tell me what happened tonight, Baby."

Baby had turned her fourth trick of the night and, in need of a fix, had wandered off the strip and into the covert protection of somebody's back yard where she'd sat down close to the chain link fence, between two of the city's large, green garbage bins. Nothing was on her mind but cooking her fix. And when that was done and the drugs injected, nothing at all was on her mind, not for a nice, long, oblivious while. She could never have told a soul, had one asked, how long her nod had lasted, but she was aware that she was coming out of it when she heard a woman's voice — one of her kind of women — call out a casual, "Hey, Sugah." There was no vocal reply, but a vehicle engine revved. By this time, Baby had struggled to her feet and was wobbling out of the yard. She saw a black truck, one of those cute, sporty ones, with the top off. Four men inside. Then she saw the woman walking toward the men. Then one of the men, in the front, stood up and raised his arm, as if to wave to the woman. But there was something else . . . something sailing in the air . . . and suddenly the woman was on the ground. Baby heard another sound — a scream — close to her, too close, so close it hurt her ears. The sound reverberated in her ears. Then the man who was still standing up in the truck turned around and said something, loud words. Then the two men in the back of the cute truck stood up and they were all pointing . . .

pointing . . . at her! Suddenly the truck was backing up rapidly. Baby ran. Or rather, she turned and moved as quickly as she was able, under the circumstances. She ducked into an alley, ran about halfway through it, and slithered into an abandoned garage. She could hear the engine of the truck whining as the driver gunned it through the alley. It went fast by the garage where she hid and she instantly slid out and ran out of the mouth of the alley, on to a side street and up the block to a small bodega that she knew had a pay phone inside. The owner, a Jamaican woman, reached under the counter when Baby rushed in, then released the weapon and withdrew her hand when she recognized that the sudden opening of the door did not, this time, mean danger. She knew Baby and many of the other girls who worked the block; but more than that, she understood them. She understood because for the first several, struggling years of her life in America, she'd had to sell her body in order to live.

"What's wrong wit' you, Girl? You look like you just seen the devil." The woman had glanced intently at the door, as if expecting the devil or some other form of evil to follow Baby.

Baby had smacked a dollar on the counter. "Gimme some change, Alva, I gotta make a phone call! Quick!" Baby had snatched up the coins and rushed to the back of the store toward the beer case, to the corner where the phone was. And she remained there until she caught her breath. When she left the store, she made sure it was with her normal grin in place and her casual wave to Alva with the now-familiar admonition not to let the bastards get her down.

Mimi watched and listened as Baby ate and talked, and noticed that Baby didn't flinch when Mimi directed the waitress to bring more waffles, juice and milk.

"So I know they saw me," Baby said, finishing her story and her meal. "But they think we all look alike anyway, so I ain't really worried. Besides, I saw them, too, so if they fuck with me, you can put 'em in the newspaper, right?"

"Does that mean you can identify them, Baby?" Mimi refused to allow herself to be hopeful. Just coming out of a nod, Baby wouldn't have recognized her own mother.

"Naw. All white boys look alike to me, just like we all look alike to them. But I know the tag number of that truck."

Mimi's surprise was all over her face. "You know the license number of the black Jeep?"

"I just said so, didn't I?" Baby was getting testy. "And I seen on TV that you can find out who they are if you have the tag number. So you can just tell 'em to leave me alone."

Mimi fished her notepad and pen out of her pocket and slid it across the table to Baby, asking her to write down the tag number. Mimi didn't want any possibility of a mistake. Baby would write it as she remembered it. But to Mimi's surprise, she recoiled from the pen and pad and a sullen look replaced the smug look that had been on her face.

"Baby, what's wrong?" Mimi asked with concern.

"Nothin'," Baby replied shortly.

"I only asked you to write it because I didn't

want to make a mistake," Mimi began to explain, but Baby cut her off.

"If you write it like I tell you, won't be no mistake."

"All right," Mimi said, reaching for the offending items. She opened the pad and held the pen poised and ready.

Baby squeezed her eyes shut. "The numbers was seven, seven, nine," she said slowly. "And the other part was like my name." She sat with her eyes tightly shut, brow wrinkled in concentration.

"What do you mean, like your name?" Mimi was confused.

"My name is Marlene Jefferson. The other part was like that. Like Michael Jackson, like Michael Jordan. You know?" Baby managed to sound both plaintive and patronizing at the same time.

Mimi stumbled over the concept for a moment before realization dawned. "You mean M-J, like your initials? Those were the letters in the license plate?"

"Ain't that what I just said?" Baby Doll snarled.

Mimi's patience snapped and she was on the verge of an acid retort when she suddenly understood the reason for Baby's elaborate charade: the child could not read. Mimi's admiration for the Baby Doll increased another several points, and she again cursed the scourge that was drugs. Marlene Jefferson is, she told herself, too beautiful, too smart, and too young, to be usurped by the evil that is heroin.

Both Mimi and Baby were silent on the drive downtown. Baby would tell Mimi only that she lived somewhere off Thirteenth Street in the Columbia

Heights section of town. So when Mimi crossed the intersection of Park Road and Thirteenth Street, Baby told her to pull over. She opened the door and got out of the car, making sure to claim her wig and her wardrobe.

"I'll wash your clothes and give 'em back to you."

"I'm worried about you, Baby, not some old blue jeans."

"Don't worry 'bout me, Newspaper Lady. You find them boys, you won't have to worry 'bout me." Baby was her offhand self again. She shut the car door firmly, then leaned in. "I really 'preciate you comin' to pick me up. I didn't know who else to call."

"Will you call me tomorrow, just to let me know you're all right?" Mimi was loath not to have a way to find this girl.

"I told you. Don't worry 'bout me," Baby said, and strolled off into the darkness.

Mimi sat there for several more moments, her brain on overload. The license number that Baby had given her was incomplete: it was missing the third letter. Maryland tags carried three letters and three numbers. Baby either didn't remember or, more likely, did not know how to recognize, the third letter. But that problem was easily solved. Any law enforcement agency could ID that vehicle knowing its make and model and five of the six license numbers. Her other problem was not so easily solved. She had a source who'd just witnessed a murder. Baby might not be familiar with her responsibility to report that information to the police, but Mimi certainly was. And suppose she reported it. Then what? Tell the police that her eyewitness was a heroin-addicted prostitute who'd just finished shooting up in an alley? And as preposterous as the entire scenario was, what would Gianna say if she discovered that Mimi had withheld information about a capital crime, a felony murder? Being a reporter, protecting the sanctity of a source, that was one thing. Obstructing justice, that was quite another. Mimi buried her head in her hands.

Every eye in the Think Tank was bloodshot and bleary, and beneath every reddened eye was a heavy piece of luggage. Kenny, who didn't drink, looked hung-over. Lynda and Bobby looked flat, as if someone had let all the air out of them. Tony and Tim both looked just plain mean, though Gianna knew they had different reasons for the scowls on their faces; and Tim's was made worse by the fact that he'd gotten a new, short haircut that emphasized the angles of his face. Alice looked distraught. And Eric wore a look of pure disgust. Gianna knew she looked every bit as hellish as any one of the others because she felt, in total, like they all looked.

"I am one useless piece of shit." Tony slammed the table with his hand, sloshing coffee out of his cup.

"You're not any good to me feeling sorry for yourself, Tony," Gianna said dispassionately.

"I'm not any good to anybody, especially to that girl lying over there in the morgue with that fuckin' knife in her heart."

Bobby, Kenny, Tim and Lynda all shifted their

attention to Tony, and Gianna saw their feelings shift as well. He was no longer just an interloper but a dedicated cop who was earning their respect.

"Nothing you could have done, Tony. Either of you. She wasn't killed at your stakeout." If anyone is at fault, Gianna continued to herself, it's me. I should have moved you. Dammit! I should have moved you.

"I did see something, Lieutenant," Alice said quietly, and the focus shifted to her. "A black Jeep Wrangler. But a different one. At least one with different license plates, with Maryland instead of Virginia places, because I swear to God that it was the same Jeep."

Something was swimming around in Gianna's subconscious seeking to break the surface. What was it?

"I'll put it all in my report," Alice was saying, but Gianna was hearing Sergeant Marx explain how all the boys in the club drove identical cars. The same red Trans Am. The same black Jeep Wrangler?

"What's the license number, Alice?" Gianna picked up the phone and, in a rare public display of the authority she possessed, bypassed all of the regular channels of the department and was patched in to a system that immediately gave her the name of the person to whom the Jeep was registered: Thomas Haldane, the junior Senator from Alabama.

By the time Mimi finished telling Tyler everything that had happened the night before, he was hopping back and forth from foot to foot as if he had to go to the bathroom. Tyler was like a little kid when he got excited. And, like a little kid, he could go from ecstatic to downtrodden in a heartbeat, which was exactly what occurred when Mimi concluded her narrative with, "There's just one small problem."

Tyler's face crashed fifteen stories to the ground. "What."

"The license number . . ."

"I thought you made such a big deal of that Baby Doll person giving you the number —"

"I did, Tyler. But there's a missing letter —"

"Jesus, Patterson! Then you *don't* have the number!"

"Would you calm down for just a minute? I have the first two letters and the three numbers. Piece of cake for your FBI pal."

Tyler's lover was an FBI agent who occasionally did small favors for them. Tyler, however, never liked asking and Mimi never minded asking, so she said she'd be happy to call Don if Tyler was too chicken-shit to do it. He snatched the paper from her with the partial license number on it and stalked across the newsroom to his desk.

Mimi was on the phone to the Medical Examiner's office, trying to get some information on the murdered prostitute, when Tyler's shadow crossed her desk. He dropped the paper on which she'd written the license number, and stood waiting. She saw that the missing letter of the number had been added in red ink. Beneath the name and also in red ink the words, *THOS. HALDANE, US SENATOR, ALABAMA.*

She looked up at Tyler and couldn't read the expression in his eyes, but she knew exactly what the sinking feeling in her gut signified. She rushed through her conversation with the deputy ME and hung up. A United States senator. Jesus H. Christ on a raft, where was this story going. She allowed herself a final moment of indecision, then picked up the phone and punched in the familiar numbers.

"Lieutenant Maglione."

"I need to talk to you right away. About the murder last night. Baby saw it."

Gianna paused only the briefest second before she said, "Tell me when and where to meet you."

"At the gym," Mimi said, "in an hour."

At that time of the day, they had the steam room to themselves. Encompassed by the dark, quiet, soothing heat, Mimi told Gianna everything she'd found out about the murders of the prostitutes, including what Sandra King's mother had said about killing girls being part of some kind of an initiation rite, and concluding with what Baby saw and the license number that, if correct, meant that the junior senator from Alabama or somebody related to him had killed a prostitute.

Gianna was silent for a long moment before she

said, "It's not the senator. It's his son. And you are one hell of a good investigator, Patterson."

And then she told Mimi everything she knew about the case, including what she'd learned about Todd Haldane, Errol Allyne, Clarke Andrews, and Jerome Wilson from Sergeant Marx in Fairfax County. "You should check with him, and with the Montgomery County people. You can get access to everything but their juvenile records, and that won't matter, because these boys have been bad for a long time."

"And what, Gianna, should I do with all this information?" Mimi asked carefully. They both remembered what had happened the last time Mimi broke a major story in the middle of one of Gianna's major investigations.

"Do everything you would normally do to check your facts, confirm your sources, whatever it is you do. I will let you know when we're ready to make arrests —"

"It'll take me at least a week to pull all these pieces together, maybe longer," Mimi said.

"And it'll take us that long to obtain search warrants and arrest warrants . . ."

"Then, it'll take me two days to write the thing," Mimi whined, because writing a massive investigative story was always the hardest part.

"So," Gianna concluded, "I don't see how anything you're doing affects or interferes with anything I'm doing."

"So," Mimi said, extending her hand. "Truce?"

Gianna took her hand, returned the powerful grip, then pulled her fiercely into her arms and into her mouth.

"I love you, Mimi Patterson," Gianna whispered, her mouth still claiming Mimi's.

"As well you should," Mimi began with a laugh that was quickly replaced by the sounds of passion.

Investigations, Gianna wearily concluded, whether by police or reporters, were composed largely of activities best described as tedious, monotonous, boring and, quite often, unproductive. Investigations required following dozens of loose threads through hopelessly entangled mazes, often with the result that they led nowhere. They just came to an end. Sometimes a thread might lead to another thread, which would lead to another maze, which would then lead nowhere. Investigators also relied heavily on hunches. And investigators relied heavily on luck. And when combined — the threads and the hunches and the luck — the investigators were able to reap rewards often enough to keep them from despairing. That combination was what gave Gianna her first real hope of having a case against the boys, because, in truth, all she had was a stack of circumstantial evidence, none of it sufficient to take to a grand jury. Until the report from the police in a little town in Virginia, on the West Virginia border, where the owner of a camping and hunting store remembered selling a dozen six-inch buck knives to a University of Virginia student.

Gianna re-read the report with a sense of

satisfaction. The camping store owner was suspicious of a purchase of twelve knives by one person. His regular customers were people who knew and loved the mountains and forests and streams of that part of Virginia, people who hunted and fished and camped, people for whom a buck knife was an essential tool, a means of survival. The store owner, a man in his seventies, was also resentful of the influx of city people and their city ways into the no longer secluded and remote backwoods hamlets nestled against the Shenandoah Mountains. So the owner had questioned the purchase and was told that the knives were for members of a club called The Head Honchos. Yes, the owner would recognize the purchaser again, and he certainly would recognize his truck again: one of those fancy Jeeps, black with lots of silver and three sets of headlights and license plates from Virginia, the number the store owner just happened to jot down, mostly because he didn't trust citified boys in fancy trucks who bought knives by the boxful. The Jeep was registered to General Jefferson Davis Andrews of McLean, Virginia.

Gianna had lost count of how many times during this investigation she had wondered how and why these boys had gone so wrong so early. They'd had the best of everything, beginning with education — which is where the boys had met each other. Even though they lived in different parts of the wealthy Maryland and Virginia suburbs that surrounded Washington, the boys had all attended the same exclusive prep school in D.C., beginning in the first grade. All of them were intelligent, good students, active in social and academic clubs and societies. But the propensity for violence had begun early. Why?

Perhaps, Gianna thought, that was a question best left to the Beverlys of the world; for in truth, Gianna didn't care why. She only wanted to put Todd Haldane and Clarke Andrews and Jerome Wilson and Errol Allyne in jail for a very long time. Maybe somebody there could find out why the boys thought it was all right to kill women for sport. What she wanted was to place them in Todd Haldane's Jeep on the night of October third in an alley between Eleventh and Twelfth Streets in northwest Washington. And to do that she'd need more than Marlene Jefferson, aka Baby Doll.

She opened the file on Todd Haldane, though she knew every word contained there as well as every word in each of the other files. And what she knew was that the Haldane boy was not like the others. He was a follower, a tag-along. Haldane got in trouble because the other boys did, because he wanted to be part of the in-crowd. And nothing in the background information on the Alabama senator suggested that he was the same kind of violent bully as General Andrews. The Haldane boy had not participated in the rape or in any of the other violent incidents. He was present, yes, but usually drunk. So maybe if they leaned on Haldane, really leaned on him and on his senator father . . .

Eric was leaning on store and shop owners on Tenth and Eleventh and Twelfth and O and P and Q Streets with absolutely no success. Despite the fact that the Chinese carry-out and the candy and cigarette store and the gas station were open all night, not a single person admitted to having seen or heard anything unusual the night before last. Several even claimed not to have heard the sirens of the police cruisers and ambulances. None was concerned enough or interested enough to investigate the flashing lights. Only one admitted to being too frightened to leave the safety of his store to find out what was going on. But, disgust notwithstanding, Eric continued to methodically criss-cross his way through the area. He must find someone to corroborate what Baby Doll said she saw.

The bell over the door tinkled when Eric opened it, and he stood there looking around until Alva casually worked her way up to the front of the store.

"What you want, Mr. P'liceman? And don' ask me how I know you th' p'lice. I ain't stupid, you know."

Eric grinned at her, at the truth of her words as much as at the lovely, lilting sound her voice made, the warmth of the Caribbean resonating in it. "A woman was murdered in the alley . . ."

"I know. Poor t'ing." Alva shook her head and clucked her teeth. "When you people gonna stop such?"

"When are you people gonna help us? I wasn't in the alley that night, but somebody was, and until we locate . . ."

"Well, I know who was but she ain't gonna talk to the likes of you." Alva put her hands on her narrow hips and looked Eric up and down.

He let her complete her sizing up of him, then asked, "And are you gonna talk to the likes of me?"

"One of th' girls run in here to use the phone. Scared white she was. No offense, Mr. P'liceman. Then she waits for a while. Then she leaves. I go out after her, just to make sure she's okay, you know? 'Cause she's a good girl."

"Baby Doll?" Eric asked.

"Ah, so you know 'bout Baby. Then you know 'bout them white boys that was after her."

"Tell me about them," Eric asked.

And Alva told him about the little black truck with the four white men that tried to follow Baby but couldn't because she kept darting in and out of doorways and alleys. Alva lost sight of her, too, and returned to her store. Then she heard all the sirens and went back out to see what was happening.

"That's when I saw that little red car. Baby was in it with another lady — real pretty t'ing she was, and not no workin' girl neither — and the little black truck was followin' 'em."

Little red car. Montgomery Patterson. *And the little black truck was following the little red car.* Which meant that Baby Doll would not be the only target of the boys' revenge. The Lieutenant would go ballistic when Eric told her.

But one look at the Lieutenant's face, and Eric decided to postpone telling her anything resembling bad news. She'd spent the morning at the hospital with Cassie, helping to tell her what had happened to her and why, and why she didn't remember and why it was possible that she would never see from her left eye again. Then Gianna had had the identical conversation with Cassie's parents. Then she'd held Cassie while the girl wept and wondered what she'd done to deserve such punishment. And by the time

Gianna finished convincing the young officer that the sick, evil acts of human beings could in no way be construed to be Divine punishment or retribution — "God doesn't hurt people, Cassie. People hurt each other —" the superior officer was completely drained. She barely had enough energy remaining to review all the reports that had come in in the last twenty-four hours, including Eric's on Alva.

"Good work," Gianna said. "Will she recognize them again?"

"The truck for sure. She wrote down the tag number. And maybe the boy in the passenger seat. She said he had red hair like mine, though not as pretty."

And Gianna smiled with Eric and the others at the little bit of much needed levity. Eric deliberately omitted what Alva had told him about the boys in the black truck following the red car, and the danger he believed that posed for Montgomery Patterson. He'd take care of that himself.

Mimi had never been so warmly received by a police officer as she was received by Sergeant Danny Marx of the Fairfax County Police when she told him what she wanted. He brightened even more when she told him she'd been briefed by Lieutenant Maglione, off the record, of course. Of course, Sergeant Marx responded expansively. And his comments would have to be off the record, as well, but he'd tell her whatever she wanted to know. "I read your stuff in the paper, Miss Patterson, and you do damn fine work." And when he'd answered her every question with more detail than she'd dared hope for, he'd given her the name of a Montgomery County, Maryland officer who, he assured her, would be just as pleased to talk to her. Mimi thanked Marx and let him know that if she could ever return the favor, he need only call. Cops and reporters coexisted peacefully to the extent that they could help each other. Sometimes it was a news story that broke a case for the cops, a carefully worded, well-planted news story. Mimi knew that and so did Marx — that's why he was talking to her. The police hadn't been able to nail Clarke Andrews and his pals; maybe the press could. She gathered up her notes and tape recorder, placed it all in her briefcase, and extended her hand to Marx.

She was putting on her jacket when he said, "You know the little bastards used to wear jackets that had a serpent emblem — that was their logo — and their name."

"I didn't know that," Mimi said surprised. "What was their name?"

"The Head Honchos. Can you believe that?"

Mimi could believe it, after everything she'd just heard. She was on her way to the door when Marx killed all the good feelings she had for him.

"That Lieutenant Maglione. I, ah, checked her out, just to know who I was dealing with, you know?"

Mimi turned a cold, steady gaze on Sergeant Marx. "And?"

"And, well, I just wondered how well you know her."

"I know her," Mimi said shortly. "Why?"

"Well, is she married?" Marx finally asked, and Mimi laughed.

"Yeah, Sergeant, I believe she is," Mimi said, halfway out of the door, still laughing.

"Well," Marx called out after her, "how about you? You married?"

"Yeah, I believe I am, too."

And Mimi grinned to herself all the way back on the pretty drive out Route 66 to the George Washington Parkway, along the Potomac, and into Washington. She took the long route because fall was in full bloom and the trees were changing clothes for the season, having gotten out their reds and oranges and golds. This beauty could always overcome the ugliness of the lives human beings made for themselves.

Mimi was politely if not warmly received by Detective John Butler in the Gaithersburg station of the Montgomery County Police. Sergeant Marx had already called him, and he'd already spoken to Lieutenant Maglione, whom he knew, and if Lieutenant Maglione would talk to a reporter, so would he. And talk he did, actually divulging more information than had Sergeant Marx, because from Butler Mimi learned that two of the boys — Errol Allyne and one whose name she'd not heard before, Geoffrey Greene — had been arrested and charged just two years ago for killing and dismembering neighborhood cats. They used, Butler said, hunting knives.

"Who is Geoffrey Greene? I don't have his name."

"That's because his father is the chief judge of the circuit court," Butler said sourly.

And instead of being elated at the prospect of yet another son of yet another prominent man, Mimi felt only a dull heaviness, and along with it, the realization that she'd feel no thrill when she saw this story on the front page of the paper, topped by her byline.

Eric was too tired to be pissed off at Tim's brusque refusal to meet him, Kenny, and Bobby at Armand's for pizza and beer. He was busy, Tim said, and stalked off. They'd all been dismayed at Gianna's description of Cassie's condition, at the fact that she would not be able to identify her attackers because she didn't remember the attack. But Tim was acting as if it were their fault. Dammit, didn't he understand that all of them hurt? He, Eric, and Kenny and Bobby? Tim wasn't the only one of them to feel the loss of Cassie, not to mention what that loss had done to the other women in the Unit — to the Boss and to Lynda. Nobody talked about it but it was there. Not only were they vulnerable as cops, they were vulnerable as women.

"Shit," Eric said glumly to his beer. Then he looked up at Bobby and Kenny and told them about Montgomery Patterson's car being followed by the black Jeep and how he thought it was possible that the reporter was in danger and how he wondered if they were game for an off-the-books surveillance of

Patterson's residence until somebody was busted for the hooker murders.

"I'm game, but why off-the-books?" Kenny asked.

Eric answered carefully. "Because I don't want to cause the Lieutenant any unnecessary worry."

"Red Karmann Ghia convertible. Why does that ring a bell?" Bobby asked. "Has that vehicle ever been part of a case file?"

"Not that I'm aware of," Eric answered, still careful.

"Yeah, sounds familiar to me, too," Kenny said.

"Miss Patterson is a friend of the Lieutenant's," Eric said.

And the lights went on for Bobby and Kenny. Cassie, describing the woman she believed to be the Lieutenant's lover and the red Karmann Ghia convertible the woman drove.

"Fuck a duck," Bobby muttered under his breath, in imitation of his boss.

"Son of a bitch," Kenny whispered.

"So since it appears that you both understand the relevance of securing Miss Patterson's safety, here's what I propose."

And Eric detailed a plan that would post one of them — Eric, Kenny or Bobby — outside the Patterson residence all night every night. The surveillance vehicle would be Eric's new Blazer with its tinted windows and cellular phone. They would, of course, be expected to perform their other duties as usual, which meant excruciating fatigue would be the order of the day. When both Kenny and Bobby nodded their agreement, Eric again was irritated at Tim's dismissal of him. With four of them rotating surveillance, it meant that one of them would have to be awake for almost twenty-four hours every fourth day instead of every third day. Well, maybe he'd try talking to Tim tomorrow . . .

"Suppose they try it, Eric," Bobby said quietly. "Suppose one of those fuckers tries to throw a knife into the Lieutenant's . . . ah . . . into the Patterson woman. What do we do?"

"Blow his goddamn brains out," Eric said.

XII

Mimi thought the ringing phone was a part of her dream, or perhaps a part of someone else's dream, it sounded so far away. And besides, somewhere deep within her unconscious mind, she refused to accept that the middle-of-the-night ringing of the phone could become a habit. Gianna, on the other hand, awakened immediately, reached across Mimi to pick up the phone on the second ring, and put it to Mimi's face.

"Answer the phone, Mimi," she hissed in that instantly awake state that Mimi hated.

"Hullo," Mimi mumbled.

"I'm sorry to bother you, Miss Patterson. This is Detective Ashby . . ."

Now Mimi was awake. "Just a moment, Detective," she said, sitting up and passing the phone to Gianna and whispering to her that it was Eric Ashby. Mimi switched on the light and saw that all the color had drained from Gianna's face.

"Eric? What's wrong?"

"You'd better get over here right away. It's Tim . . ."

"Tim!" Gianna gasped. "What's wrong with Tim and get over where?" she snapped as she grabbed the pen and pad Mimi gave her. She quickly wrote down an address in the middle of a groan that turned into a whispered curse. "I'm on my way," she said as she slammed down the phone. She didn't move for a moment, and neither did Mimi.

Then Gianna turned to face her. "It seems that Officer McCreedy took it upon himself to go undercover to locate Cassie's assailants."

"And did he locate them?" Mimi asked carefully.

"Oh, yes, he located them. Though there may not be much of them left to prosecute." Gianna climbed slowly out of bed and went to the closet. "I need clothes," she said, grabbing a pair of Mimi's jeans and a shirt.

"Gianna . . ." Mimi began hesitantly.

"Come on, Patterson," Gianna said, usurping her thought. "You up to an exclusive story this morning?"

They were dressed and out the door in less than three minutes. They took Gianna's unmarked police sedan and while Gianna drove — lights flashing but no siren — Mimi used the car phone to call Tyler and she shocked Gianna silly when she advised him to call night city editor Henry Smith and have a reporter and photographer sent to cover the arrest of the neo-Nazis who would be charged with the assault on Officer Cassandra Ali.

"You're giving the story away?" Gianna asked, disbelief unmasked in her voice.

Mimi shrugged. "I can work any ol' time. I thought that tonight — this morning, rather — I'd just stand around and be supportive. In case you needed a supportive, uninvolved partner standing around, that is."

Gianna took her hand. "Did I happen to mention how much I love you?"

"Not in the last three or four hours."

"Well, I do," Gianna said.

"You do what?" Mimi challenged.

"I do love you, and anything else you think you want."

"That'll do. For now."

Mimi closed her eyes and leaned her head back on the seat, thinking she'd grab a few moments of sleep on the cross-town journey. Until Gianna switched on the siren and accelerated the powerful engine. Mimi lurched forward and, eyes wide open now, watched as the traffic parted, watched as Gianna expertly maneuvered the speeding vehicle, watched as Gianna underwent the transformation of becoming the Lieutenant.

It took less than fifteen minutes to get all the way downtown to a grungy, ugly area of Southeast, south of but in sight of the Capitol dome, into an industrial area that Mimi knew was home to several gay bars, as well as to a sprawling public housing project. What would neo-Nazi skinheads be doing in an area like this? But there they were, four of them lined up against a police cruiser, three of them in handcuffs. Gianna screeched the car to a halt between two other police cruisers, slammed the gear into park, put on the brake, opened the door and got out, all in one fluid motion, before Mimi had even opened her door.

Gianna stalked over to a small knot of men, including four that Mimi had identified as belonging to a neo-Nazi group because of their heavy black leather jackets and boots and severely short haircuts. Surprisingly, two of the men seemed familiar to Mimi: one, sullen and sallow with several deep scratches on his face and blood flowing from his nose; and the other tall, muscular, with bleached blond, almost white hair, in a buzz cut. He looked fiercely angry.

Mimi watched Gianna, watched her responses to the two men who had attracted Mimi's attention. Gianna did a double-take when she saw the blond, then stared at him so intently that the anger left the man's face and he lowered his eyes, almost in shame. Neither of them spoke.

Then Gianna turned to the other man, the one with the scratches on his face and the bloody nose. She walked to within a foot of him and he said something and Gianna backed up a step. He said something else and Gianna slapped him with every ounce of power in her body. Then she backhanded him, again with such force that Mimi was certain she must have hurt herself.

Mimi decided not to worry about the consequences

and hurried over to Gianna. In that instant, two other men moved in, Eric Ashby and one she didn't recognize, each taking Gianna by an arm and leading her away. Mimi saw the pain and anger in her face and wanted to be near her, but she also knew better than to get in the way of Gianna's work. She retreated, walking back to stand next to Gianna's car where she could see all that happened and be nearby, just in case, but where she also was well out of the way, both of the police and of the reporter, to whom she had no desire to explain her presence.

Gianna pulled free of Eric and the detective in charge of the investigation. "I don't need to be restrained," she snapped.

"There's a reporter here," Eric said quietly.

"I know that," Gianna snapped again before she understood that he was not talking about Mimi. She got her anger under control and turned toward Tim.

He met her gaze and came toward her. She was amazed at the transformation in him. In the black studded leather jacket with his hair bleached and the earring, he looked so much like the real thing that he made her uncomfortable. "Care to explain yourself, McCreedy?"

Tim winced, took a deep breath, and launched into his explanation which, quite simply, was that with Cassie unlikely to ever remember who assaulted her, it was important to find the perps before their wounds healed; otherwise, there would be no way to tell one of them from the other. Tim said he knew that a lot of the pseudo-Nazis — "I call 'em that because they don't really believe in anything but violence. They're not political, just evil —" were a peripheral part of the leather scene. They were heavy into sado-masochism and didn't care who they had sex with as long as it was rough. Which was why, Tim believed, he would eventually find Cassie's attackers at the roughest, sleaziest, leather bar in town, the Rough Trade Brigade. Tim said he'd seen the one with the scratches all over his face for the first time three nights ago, but he was alone.

"I knew all I had to do was wait and he'd bring the others. So, I bought him a beer and talked a lot about hating queers, Jews, niggers, and the government." Tim shrugged and nodded toward the three men now wearing handcuffs, courtesy of the Metropolitan Police Department, instead of the Rough Trade Brigade. "I just hope one of 'em will roll over and give up the one who Cassie shot."

Gianna, still grim-faced, turned to look at Jack Tolliver, the one with the deep scratches down both sides of his face. Jack Tolliver, whom she'd questioned as a part of a murder investigation a year and a half ago. Jack Tolliver, whose face said he'd done horrible things to Cassandra Ali.

"One of 'em will roll over," Gianna said flatly.

"Lieutenant —" Tim began.

But she cut him off. "We'll talk later, Tim." She was in no mood to think about how to handle him, especially since she had herself just violated a whole section of the code book by assaulting Tolliver.

She went over to talk to the detective in charge of the case, to offer her assistance if needed, and to ascertain, without stepping on his toes, how he would treat Tim in his report.

"You tell me how you want it handled, Lieutenant, and that's how I'll handle it."

"I respect your judgment, Detective."

Gianna breathed relief. Tim would be safe, at least until she got around to dealing with him.

"And just in case you were wondering," the detective added quietly, "nobody saw you hit that piece of dog shit, including the newspaper reporter."

Gianna raised her eyebrows but she did not speak the question. "The reporter owes me, Lieutenant," the detective drawled, and left her standing there rubbing the hand that was beginning to throb. She made a fist and winced at the sharp pain that shot up her arm.

"Everything okay?" Eric said from behind her.

"If I haven't broken my hand, yes," she said wearily.

"What should I do with McCreedy?"

"Send him home to bed," she answered, "and you go home to bed, and I'm going home to bed —" She stopped and frowned. "Speaking of which, why did you call me at Mimi's?" That had been tugging at her ever since the phone rang.

"Because you weren't home and I assumed that . . . anyway, I'd rather use the phone than the beeper," he finished lamely, and then began to fidget when she fixed him in her hazel stare.

"You're full of it, Ashby, but I'm too tired to deal with it." And, stifling a yawn, she waved at the detective in charge, and walked slowly to her car, where Mimi was standing, waiting.

Mimi noticed that Gianna winced in pain when she switched on the ignition, and when she shifted gears, but she kept silent. Nor did she comment when she noticed that Gianna was driving with her left hand. What she said was, "Who was the guy you hit? Why did he look familiar?"

"Remember the demonstration outside Freddie's? The Can You Keep a Secret people?"

And it all came back to Mimi and they talked about that case for a few moments. Then Mimi said, "So. Did you break your hand?"

"Maybe," Gianna said quietly.

"Wanna go see Cassie?" Mimi asked.

And Gianna, using her left hand to steer, changed direction and pointed the car toward the Washington Hospital Center, smiling inwardly at how well Mimi Patterson was learning to handle her.

The junior senator from Alabama was a tall, strikingly handsome man with coal-black hair flecked with silver, light gray eyes topped with bushy brows, and a gentle, but deep baritone voice heavily accented with the speech patterns of his native state. Senator Thomas Haldane also possessed the courtly manners ascribed to men of the South: he was polite and courteous and expressed genuine concern when Gianna apologized for not being able to shake his hand because of the damage done to her own, which was in a cast because of the two small bones she'd broken when she'd backhanded Jack Tolliver.

Haldane invited Gianna and Eric into the white-columned colonial-style mini-mansion that was his home away from home. He led them from the foyer down a wide hallway, past a circular staircase and two sets of double French doors, to a rear sitting room, where he introduced them to Mrs. Haldane, every bit as attractive and charming as her husband, and to Todd, who possessed all of his parents' good looks and none of their charm.

Gianna had cleared her visit to Bethesda with the Montgomery County authorities, promising to keep them abreast of developments since she was on their turf, and since a public figure of some prominence was involved. Then she'd requested and gotten an arrest warrant, just in case. When she'd called Haldane to arrange the meeting, she'd been prepared to execute the warrant then and there, remembering Sergeant Marx's description of General Andrews; but Haldane had been too disbelieving to be defensive. He was still disbelieving.

"I must tell you, Lieutenant, that it is not possible that Todd is involved in what you suggest."

"I believe he is, Senator, which is why I recommended that you and your wife be present, and why I also suggested that you might wish to consult an attorney."

"I am an attorney, Lieutenant —"

Gianna cut him off. "Are you a criminal lawyer, Senator?"

"I am not." He bristled for the first time. "Nor do I need to be. My son has done nothing wrong."

Gianna shifted her gaze and her focus from the senator to his son and shocked them both. "You have the right to remain silent. Anything you say can and will be used against you in a court of law. You have the right to speak to an attorney —"

"For God's sake, Thomas, do something!" Mrs. Haldane was the first to understand fully the implications of Gianna's words, and she rushed to her son's side. The boy clung to his mother and tears filled his eyes.

"Surely that's not necessary," the senator exclaimed, rising to tower over Gianna.

"I told you that this was a criminal investigation, Senator," Gianna said coldly. To which Haldane responded just as coldly, "Then I withdraw permission for Todd to be interrogated."

Instead of replying, Gianna reached into her shoulder bag and removed the arrest warrant, which she silently gave to Haldane. The scowl of anger on his face turned to fear and he backed up a few steps and looked helplessly at his wife, who looked helplessly at Gianna.

"What do you want Todd to tell you?" Mrs. Haldane asked.

"Do you give up your right to remain silent, Todd?" He shrugged, wiped the tears from his eyes, and nodded. Gianna began the questioning.

"Do you have a drinking problem, Todd?"

Clearly startled by the question, he stuttered and stammered before he was able to answer. "Yeah, I guess so," he mumbled.

"How bad is it?"

"Pretty bad, I guess."

"Were you too drunk to drive last Friday night?"

"No," he said positively.

"So you were driving your Jeep yourself? Not Clarke, or Geoff, or Errol?"

"I never let anybody drive my Jeep."

"So you were driving when Geoff threw the knife?"

Todd's eyes grew wide and he swallowed hard

several times and he opened his mouth to speak but no words would come out.

"Is that the first time you drove when somebody threw the knife?"

The black Jeep had been twice around the block, slowing to a crawl each time it came abreast of Mimi's house, then speeding up to go past. Eric couldn't tell who was driving or how many were inside. On the third pass-by, the passenger door opened and an arm emerged and flailed in the air, then the Jeep lurched forward and was half way down the block before Eric heard the shattering of glass. Fuckin' tinted windows! Why did he get tinted windows? What glass was shattered? He peered through every window in the Blazer, front, back, side. No sign of the Jeep.

Then an upstairs light went on in the house and, several seconds later, a downstairs light went on and almost immediately, the front porch light came on.

Eric's stomach tightened. He unsnapped his gun and freed it from the holster.

The front door of the house opened and he could clearly see Mimi Patterson silhouetted in the doorway, wearing a long, multi-colored caftan. Then she stepped out onto the porch and walked to the right of the house and leaned in toward the window.

That's when he saw the shadow move. That's when he moved. He flipped open the door of the truck and hurled himself onto the sidewalk, remaining in a crouch and close to the truck.

The woman returned to her front door and, fully

illuminated, stood staring at the shattered front window. That was when the shadow straightened and when Eric shouted and when the shadow threw something and when the woman whirled and ducked and when Eric raised his arm and fired once, twice, and then the shadow fell.

Tires screeched and an engine whined and the black Jeep roared off down the street. A dog barked. A dying boy groaned. A dispirited, disheartened woman wept softly. A grimly satisfied police detective sighed heavily. Night songs.

Mimi wrote nonstop for two and a half days. Tyler spent the time standing over her, proofreading literally every word as fast as it appeared on the computer screen. She was so drained of emotion that his hovering didn't annoy her, which caused him to worry about her health.

"Patterson, are you sure you're all right?"

"I will have a fit and die on the spot if you ask me that again, Tyler. I'm just wonderful, okay?"

While Mimi would never know what instinct caused her duck when she heard Eric shout, she also would never forget the sight of the buck knife embedded in her front door at just about the level where her throat had been the instant before. So, technically, yes, she was okay. She wasn't dead, so she was okay. But something inside her would never be the same again. Whatever that thing was, it was related to the thing that was missing while she wrote the story ... and it was the thing that had always made her antsy and edgy and excited while she wrote a major story.

During the two and a half days that she wrote about the Head Honchos and the ten women they had murdered in the spring and the fall of the year as a ritualistic part of their own secret society, she felt almost no emotion. She wrote because writing was what she knew how to do. She wrote in an orderly, logical, methodical fashion because that's how she was trained. And the story she wrote was, according to all her editors, brilliant.

But she didn't care. It didn't matter, and her narrow escape from the knife expertly thrown by Clarke Andrews was not the reason it didn't matter. Strangely enough, what mattered to her was that Clarke Andrews had died on her front lawn. He was a twenty-one-year-old murderer who, if he hadn't been killed, would likely have spent the remainder of his life in jail. That would have been all right, she thought. But it was not all right that he was dead, that his blood was fertilizing her grass. Carolyn King was glad he was dead, since he was the one who had killed her daughter. Gwen Thomas was glad he was dead, since he was the one who had killed her sister. But Mimi was not glad he was dead. And she didn't know why. She knew only that she experienced no pride, no rush of satisfaction when her story led to the military's investigation of General Andrews and the Maryland Attorney General's investigation of Judge Greene; or when it was revealed that the fathers of all the boys had conspired to protect their sons from the consequences of their actions. Indeed, after she wrote the initial two stories, Mimi wanted nothing to do with the multitude of follow-up stories. And it wasn't until she was reading one of those stories that Mimi began to understand the source of the ennui that enveloped her. It was the story in which the photographs of all the murdered women appeared and it suddenly struck Mimi that they all were Black. Black like her. And she allowed herself to feel fully the pain of knowing that there were people who believed her life had no value because of her race.

Tyler wrote the sidebar story to Mimi's lead story, the story in which it was explained how it happened that Clarke Andrews came to die in a reporter's front yard; how it happened that the reporter became a target in the first place and how the elite Hate Crimes Unit surveillance saved her life; how it happened that the reporter had befriended the young prostitute. A wonderful, heart-warming story, all the other editors said.

Baby said it was bullshit, but then Baby couldn't read, so her literary criticism didn't matter a lot. What mattered was that Baby, who now insisted upon being called Marlene, was having serious talks with Sylvia about getting off drugs, about seeing Beverly for counseling, and about learning to read. Baby . . . ah, Marlene, made it clear that she hadn't committed to anything, but what the hell, it didn't hurt to talk about it. She also made it clear that eating vegetables was not part of the discussion.

Neither was there joy resounding within the walls of the Think Tank. Relief, yes. The members of the

Hate Crimes Unit tried to outdo each other with tales of how many hours, how many consecutive days, they'd slept without interruption. And when they weren't competing with each other about sleeping, they were competing with each other about whose turn it was to spend time with Cassie, who had moved in temporarily with Tim, to the audible dismay of half a dozen specimens of male pulchritude. Cassie, whose body was healing but whose spirit remained damaged and fragile. Cassie, who, as she began to remember bits and pieces of what happened to her, became more and more withdrawn, and resembled less and less the feisty, wisecracking, cynical conscience of the Hate Crimes Unit. Cassie, who also was talking to Beverly because she'd taken an instant and intense dislike to the Police Department psychiatrist; and Bev wondered cryptically what Mimi and Gianna had done with their "special cases" before there was such a thing as Midtown Psychotherapy Associates.

Gianna, when given the option, decided to remain a cowboy.

She'd adapted well to the free-wheeling life of the elite units and, though she still surprised herself with how easily she'd learned to break rules she'd never have bent before, she was learning to like the freedom. She liked the feeling when she arrested General Andrews, especially after Tim had had to break the man's arm when he'd thrown a punch at Gianna. She liked the feeling of rounding up the parents of the other Head Honchos and bringing them in for questioning — if General Andrews was an accessory, other parents probably were — though she would not soon forget the anguish of Todd Haldane's parents or the pathetic relief of General Andrews's wife when she finally understood that she had been freed from her basement prison. She liked the feeling of confiscating the black Jeep Wranglers, of issuing the search warrants for the expensive homes in the suburbs and for the rooms in the college dormitories. She liked finding the knives and the practice targets: torsos with the hearts outlined in red.

But no matter how much satisfaction she took in the various elements of solving the most complex case of her career, the hollow feeling that was carved into her when she saw the knife sticking out of Mimi's door just wouldn't be filled. She'd never forget screeching up to Mimi's house that night — Eric had sent Tim to get her — and seeing the body under the plastic tarp on the ground and even though her brain knew that Mimi was unharmed, her heart leapt. And she'd run up the walkway and there was the knife in the door . . .

No matter how closely she held Mimi, no matter how deeply she kissed her, no matter how sweetly she made love to her, there would always be the knife in the door. Just as there would always be the damage to Cassie Ali's left eye.

Gianna wrote her final report on the Head Honcho case in much the same way that Mimi had written her story: nonstop. For three days she wrote

212

and documented and wrote and documented. Hunched over the keyboard, hunting and pecking because of the right hand still in a cast, and surrounded by piles of her notes and files and daily reports. And frequently during the writing she would digress to write a memo to herself about something she wanted to remember, or to send a note to someone else — Sergeant Marx, for instance, thanking him for his help, and Adrienne Lightfoot.

And in the middle of her writing, the detective in charge of Cassie's case paid her a visit. He wanted her to read his report of the night Jack Tolliver and his cohorts were arrested. Jim Dudley was his name, and Gianna knew that whenever they crossed paths again, there would be a solid bond of respect and gratitude. Gianna and Dudley both knew that Tim had caught his perps for him . . . and they both knew that Tim's ass could be dismissed for what he did: undercover with no permission and no gun and no badge and nobody knowing where he was and all the time running the risk of blowing the entire case if he said or did anything that could remotely be construed to be entrapment, not to mention stepping all over another cop's case, not to mention endangering his own life. But they'd been lucky. Both Gianna and Dudley knew it. And so she read the report that saved Tim's ass by giving Dudley credit for the collar.

"Good collar, Detective," she said solemnly. "The entire Hate Crimes Unit owes you a debt of gratitude."

"Lieutenant, I'd go into battle with you and your people any day. Especially that Officer Ali."

Detective Dudley still couldn't get over the

damage that Cassie had inflicted upon three assailants, all the while preventing herself from being raped. Finally, Dudley left her to her report.

Having talked to him somehow helped her understand what she was feeling, helped her understand why she couldn't shake the sorrow and sadness that had settled around her. And it was more than her fear for Mimi and her anger at Cassie's disfigurement. She realized that she'd shouldered other people's pain as well: Carolyn King's and Gwen Thomas's and Eva Mae Harris's and Marlene Jefferson aka Baby Doll's and Thomas Haldane's and Sophie Gwertzman's and that of ten women who were dead because they were so hated that their lives were perceived to be without value.

Tony Watkins and Alice Long opened the door and poked their heads in. She felt a rush of joy for the first time in weeks. She was honestly glad to see them.

"Lieutenant. How's it going?" Tony asked.

"It's going, Tony. How are you?"

"Great. Thanks to you, I'm detailed to the Gangs and Violence Task Force. That's the top of the line, you know? Almost as elite as Hate Crimes."

"You talk a good game, Watkins," Gianna said grinning and shaking with her left hand the hand that he extended to her. "Thanks for your help, Tony. You made a big difference."

"It's one of the best assignments I've ever had, Lieutenant, and that's no bullshit." He tossed her a salute when he got to the door. "And I'm always available to you. I mean that. See ya, Long Legs," he said to Alice, and left the room.

Alice smiled her soft, half-smile. "How you holdin' up, Lieutenant?" she asked. "That was a bitch of a case. Never seen nothin' like it, to be honest with you."

"Neither had I, Alice. And I'm holding up really well." Gianna knew the other woman had something on her mind, and she waited until she was ready to share it.

"I know there probably never will be a good time for me to say what I want to say, so I'll just get it over with right now." She took a deep breath and looked directly, unwaveringly at Gianna. "When you start thinkin' about a replacement for Officer Ali, I hope you'll consider me." Gianna's face registered her surprise and Alice was instantly apologetic. "I didn't mean to be rude or insensitive, Lieutenant . . ."

"I know that, Alice. To tell you the truth, I suppose I'd been avoiding thinking about Cassie's situation. But eventually I will have to think about it, and when I do, you will definitely be a factor in my thinking. That's a promise."

Alice stood and offered Gianna her hand. "I appreciate it, Lieutenant. I agree with Tony. This is the best assignment I ever had."

She got almost to the door and stopped, turned, and faced Gianna, again focusing the steady gaze on her. "And just in case it makes a difference, I'm a lesbian." And Alice Long turned and left the room, left Gianna with her mouth hanging open.

XIII

Freddie and Cedric drove them to the airport. It was the third week of December and the temperature hadn't gotten out of the twenties in a week. Nobody remembered it being so cold so early in the season, and everybody was bemoaning what that portended for the approaching winter. Gianna and Mimi didn't care. They were en route to Jamaica, where they'd be until the middle of the second week in January. Freddie had made the arrangements, which included a condo on the beach at Ocho Rios, and had presented the non-refundable tickets to them at

Thanksgiving dinner. The vacation was their joint Christmas present and there was no way for them not to go without costing Freddie a small fortune. So, they were going. Gratefully, and finally, en route to the airport, with unbridled excitement.

"I'll bet you both sleep for the first three days," Cedric said, sharing their excitement.

"If I do," Mimi replied, "I'll have the worst case of sunburn in recorded history, because I intend to spend every daylight hour on the beach."

"Ditto," Gianna said, a dreamy look in her eyes. She'd been conjuring up visions of the ocean for the last week.

"Promise me you'll make love on the beach at least once," Freddie wheedled.

"I'll not promise any such thing, Fredrick Schuyler," Gianna hissed, embarrassment creeping in a red flush all over her face.

"There are private beaches," Cedric said, trying to help.

"Not that private," Gianna retorted as the three of them laughed at her.

"Don't worry," Mimi said sagely. "She'll do it. And more than once."

"Wanna bet?" Gianna challenged.

"Everything you got, Lieutenant," Mimi said decisively, taking the challenge.

And they both looked dreamily forward to collecting on that bet.

A few of the publications of
THE NAIAD PRESS, INC.
P.O. Box 10543 • Tallahassee, Florida 32302
Phone (904) 539-5965
Toll-Free Order Number: 1-800-533-1973
Mail orders welcome. Please include 15% postage.

NIGHT SONGS by Penny Mickelbury. 224 pp. A Gianna
Maglione Mystery. Second in a series.   ISBN 1-56280-097-3 $10.95

GETTING TO THE POINT by Teresa Stores. 256 pp. Classic
southern Lesbian novel.   ISBN 1-56280-100-7   10.95

PAINTED MOON by Karin Kallmaker. 224 pp. Delicious
Kallmaker romance.   ISBN 1-56280-075-2   9.95

THE MYSTERIOUS NAIAD edited by Katherine V. Forrest &
Barbara Grier. 320 pp. Love stories by Naiad Press authors.
                                              ISBN 1-56280-074-4   14.95

DAUGHTERS OF A CORAL DAWN by Katherine V. Forrest.
240 pp. Tenth Anniversay Edition.   ISBN 1-56280-104-X   10.95

BODY GUARD by Claire McNab. 208 pp. A Carol Ashton Mystery.
6th in a series.   ISBN 1-56280-073-6   9.95

CACTUS LOVE by Lee Lynch. 192 pp. Stories by the beloved
storyteller.   ISBN 1-56280-071-X   9.95

SECOND GUESS by Rose Beecham. 216 pp. An Amanda Valentine
Mystery. 2nd in a series.   ISBN 1-56280-069-8   9.95

THE SURE THING by Melissa Hartman. 208 pp. L.A. earthquake
romance.   ISBN 1-56280-078-7   9.95

A RAGE OF MAIDENS by Lauren Wright Douglas. 240 pp. A
Caitlin Reece Mystery. 6th in a series.   ISBN 1-56280-068-X   9.95

TRIPLE EXPOSURE by Jackie Calhoun. 224 pp. Romantic drama
involving many characters.   ISBN 1-56280-067-1   9.95

UP, UP AND AWAY by Catherine Ennis. 192 pp. Delightful
romance.   ISBN 1-56280-065-5   9.95

These are just a few of the many Naiad Press titles — we are the oldest and
largest lesbian/feminist publishing company in the world. Please request a
complete catalog. We offer personal service; we encourage and welcome
direct mail orders from individuals who have limited access to bookstores
carrying our publications.